For my family and friends,
who inspire me to keep writing

Dear Laurel,
Thanks for reading!
— Danny

Izena duen guzia omen da.

(That which has a name exists.)

PROLOGUE

I turned off the shower, stood in the steam, and pulled back the curtain. As I reached for my towel—darkness.

There came a warm breeze, the smell of salt, the splashy thump of waves. Sun baked my body. I was couched in sand, like a fish coated with breadcrumbs—eyes closed, muscles numb, skin roasting in the sun.

I was naked and wet, as I had been in the shower.

My eyelids parted to the sight of waves crashing on sandy beach. Sunlight stung my pupils. The ocean waves slid up to my spot in the sand—black sand. I had never seen it so dark. Pounding water, lush mountains, colorful birds.

Rising above the surf and squawk, there came a human noise, the voice of a man asking: *What's redder than blood?*

The voice was my father's.

I tried to move, to go to him. Paralysis kept me still. I was a fish coated in breadcrumbs, a body naked and wet, baking on a beach of black sand.

I pushed myself to scream. My body went cold, the sky went dark. I awoke on my bathroom floor.

* * *

I was nine years old. When I reopened my eyes, I was naked and shivering. Instead of sun there was a light bulb. Instead of sand there was linoleum. My head was pounding like ocean waves. My jaw ached. My throat tingled. My tongue scratched like sandpaper. I moved it over each of my teeth, searching nervously for gaps.

The bathroom was silent, no tidal crashing or bird noise—only the hum of the light bulb.

Dad stood in the doorway. It must have looked like a crime scene. My blood was seeping across the floor. Dad was muttering the same question I had heard him asking on the beach: *What's redder than blood?* He was stumped by his own riddle.

Mom shoved him aside and barreled in. She got down on her knees and put a hand on my head to inspect the wound.

"My God, Jax. What happened?"

"The shower. Last thing I remember was…"

Hot sun, black sand. I kept that to myself.

"Poor thing. You must have fainted."

Mom told Dad to call 9-1-1. But Dad kept his eyes on the floor, lost in the linoleum's diamond pattern. I could tell he was counting the dots and squares, double-checking to see whether the lines were random or repeating.

"Kyle," Mom insisted. "Go call for help."

"No ambulance," Dad said without looking.

Mom's eyebrows sloped into a scowl.

"Jax could have a concussion. Kyle, are you

listening to me?"

Dad shoved the fingers of his right hand through his black hair. When his hand moved over the scalp, thin lines of hair fell one by one back into place.

He turned to me. His eyes locked with mine but he was talking to Mom.

"Jax was on Ms. Jakintsu's beach."

Mom stared at him, her face tense with frustration. To her, Dad's comment was out of the blue, but there had been a beach, and I was on it.

Mom leaned down to me, her long black hair falling in front of my face. It smelled like orange peels. She kissed my forehead before taking a deep and tired breath. The breath was a heavy sigh, the sound of someone strapped with burdens.

"Look at this," she said, pointing to the bloody linoleum. "There's blood coming out of your son's head. *This* is real, Kyle. We're at home, in our bathroom. There's no beach. Now for your son's sake—and mine—go call an ambulance."

All Mom could see was my blood on the floor.

Dad clicked his heels like Dorothy in Oz—an attempt to exit this reality for a better one.

He could feel Mom's frustration. It was pooling in her dark brown eyes. She was begging him to be sensible, to fight his own brain, to do the impossible.

Dad spoke like a bad actor racing through over-rehearsed lines.

"Yes. Real. Of course. Our son is hurt. I'm going. Now. To call for help."

That night, after my head was stitched up and scanned, I found myself in the living room with Dad.

"How did you know?" I asked. "How did you know about the beach?"

He looked at me and frowned.

"This morning," I went on. "You said I went to Ms. Jakintsu's beach, remember?"

He shook his head and apologized, his face red with familiar embarrassment. He knew how his memory worked, or rather, didn't work. He knew some memories engraved themselves forever in his mind while others passed through like impatient cars at a tollbooth. The memories he wanted to keep often vanished; what he would rather forget tended to linger. Whatever thoughts he had had this morning about the beach were now tucked away in the deepest folds of his brain, inside a clump of neural mesh where no electrical signals could reach.

In time, the same would happen to me. I would also forget the beach. But to forget is not to delete. The brain is a network of roads. Some roads are highways, well traveled and relied upon. Other roads are unpaved and desolate, driven on once or twice before they are abandoned to weeds. Those roads are the kind marked with signs that read TRAVEL AT YOUR OWN RISK—which, twenty years later, is exactly what Dad and I would have to do.

CHAPTER ONE

Mom never calls midday.

My knees crack as I rise from my chair at the crowded teachers' room table.

"Hey Ma, I've got a class coming up. Can't talk now."

Ten ESL students from around the world were about to learn the second conditional by way of Tevye in *Fiddler on the Roof*.

"Jax, wait. Don't hang up."

Through the phone I hear voices muttering on intercoms. I step into the hallway and smile at passing students.

"Where are you?" I ask.

Mom speaks over the din.

"Hospital."

"What? Why? What's going on?"

"It's your sister."

"Angelica?"

I say her name like a question.

"She's injured. Badly."

A fish washed up on a beach of hot sand. My throat goes dry.

"Injured how? When?"

A few students have stopped in the hallway to listen to my conversation.

"I'm with her now."

"What happened?"

Mom takes a deep and tired breath.

"Angelica's unconscious. The doctors say she can hear, but I—I don't know."

"What do you mean you don't *know*?"

"That's just something they say. It's bad, Jax. Very bad."

Mom breathes in fast and hard through her nose, loose mucous. She's been sucking up snot in a room without tissues.

"Is Dad there?"

"Who?"

"*Dad*," I say. "Is he with you?"

"Nurse just walked in. Come to the ICU. Tell them you're my son. They'll let you in."

The chill of linoleum against bare skin.

And a voice in my head repeating a question: *What's redder than blood?*

* * *

Wax reflects overhead lights. The floor is an Impressionist's view of the ceiling. Wavy lines of reflected light glimmer underfoot like trapped ghosts. An Escher maze of halls and stairs leads me to the ICU waiting room.

A vase of daffodils stands on a coffee table. The flowers' beauty and the room's shine feel out of sync, like makeup on a corpse.

Two young boys have a play gun fight, armed

only with their index fingers and thumbs. A sobbing woman pressing a tissue to her eye hushes them.

I pick up a black phone and request access to the ICU beyond the waiting room. A nurse opens the door and sighs.

"You must be Jax."

The boys in the waiting room break from their shootout to watch me go inside.

I glance inside rooms as I pass by. In one, a man with a tube down his throat stares at the wall. He doesn't turn to look at me. Next door, a woman sleeps alone. In the window, a bouquet of flowers and a heap of linens soak up sun.

What's redder than blood?

What even is blood? Mysterious liquid: bodies make it; hearts pump it. The machinery needs no conscious instruction. Blood just flows. It can't be bought or made. When we need it, we depend on doctors, who depend on volunteers. We hope people are kind enough to donate. Where do they store donated blood? Giant vats? Refrigerated bunkers? We hear it's always in short supply, somehow, despite its ubiquity. Blood flows through humans, monkeys, dogs, parrots. There are not many types of blood, but you need the right match. Its color is a unique shade of red. You know it when you see it. Tongues and grapefruit are pinker than blood. The Red Planet is rustier. Red onions aren't even red; they're violet. And red wine is maroon like eggplant and the Dalai Lama's robe.

Red roses come close to the color of blood.

My left shoe pivots and squeaks. A nurse down the hall looks up from a clipboard. A janitor's head turns.

I enter my sister's room. Quiet beeps, no movement. The air is thick with dread. Mom wipes her watery eyes and stretches her arms out for a wordless hug. I rest my head on her shoulder, unable to speak. Her hair smells like orange peels.

Tubes connect Angelica's body to nearby machines. I can't see where the tubes meet her skin because a bed sheet covers her up, giving the illusion of comfort. The sheet hides something gruesome underneath, like a Halloween costume in reverse.

Angelica's hands lie limp at her sides, fingers curled upward, like a child reaching out to catch snowflakes. Her fingers twitch every few seconds. She is a monk in meditation, a pastor in prayer.

The attending nurse touches Angelica's bruised forehead before consulting a computer display of vital signs. Quiet beeps, no movement. Mom takes my hand and squeezes.

Suddenly I see the answer to that ridiculous question, the one that's been in my head since I got here. Angelica's polished fingernails—they are the only things redder than blood. Her nails gleam like gemstones over the bed sheet. They sting my eyes, too shiny to stare at, ruby slipper over-the-rainbow red, gaudy as Technicolor.

Though Angelica's body is bruised and bloody, her fingernails are flawless. They seem almost holy in this hopeless place. They are the proof that the person on this bed is my sister.

Red suits Angelica. It has always been her color, all the way back to the lipstick and heels she stole from Mom when we still called her Josh.

CHAPTER TWO

As far as I knew, we were two brothers on the sidewalk. But I didn't know very much.

"I want it," Josh said.

"Want what?"

We were in middle school. Dad was walking in front of us, murmuring to himself, half in our world, half in his.

Josh pointed toward the store display window, behind which hung a tall red dress.

"That's what I want." Josh was looking left and right like an undercover agent. "There, in the window."

I saw the red dress but looked for something else, anything else.

"You want *that?*"

The conversation had become subversive. The dress stayed in the window that day. It was a forbidden apple not to be picked by Josh, not yet. Dresses, lipstick, polish, heels: these things were not advertised to her body type—that is, the male body.

We talked when we got home behind a closed bedroom door.

"Josh—I just—don't get it."

The whole thing felt silly. Unreal. Impossible. Had we not shared our childhood?

"Think of it this way," my brother said. "Most women are born girls. But some aren't. They're born boys. It just happens. And I'm pretty sure it happened to me."

"Pretty sure?"

"Very sure."

"Like, *really* sure?"

"Yes."

"Is that even possible?"

"Well—yeah. Hello."

A million questions too abstract to ask. No time for me to grasp what to her was so obvious. No place for me to hide.

She was waiting for me to speak, so I stitched some words together to form a question.

"Do you think you're—like—gay?"

"This is different."

The more Josh said, the more confused I felt. He was my brother, my blood. We had gotten chicken pox together, gone to the same schools, been raised by the same parents. We shared so many things—toys, clothes, friends, genes.

How could I not have known?

* * *

She wouldn't tell our parents for another year. I told her she would get beat up if she wore a dress to school, which might have been true, or not. But I knew I didn't want to see my brother in a dress. I was afraid of how Mom and Dad would react, especially Dad. Though maybe it wouldn't be so hard for Dad. He was used to having his reality altered.

Once, he told me Ms. Jakintsu gave him a Mexican figurine.

"No," I had said before he could finish his thought. "Ms. Jakintsu isn't real, remember?"

He looked for his coffee.

Whenever he sat down there was always coffee nearby. The rituals that made up his coffee consumption—the reach for the cup, the wafting with his nose on the rim, and the long sip—it all felt like a defense mechanism, a way to stall, to give himself time to think up something to say.

"You know, Jax," he started, putting down his coffee, "people thought the Earth was the center of the universe until Copernicus said it circled the sun. They thought he was hallucinating. They called him a heretic. Can you blame them? He was changing reality. That's how they felt. But reality wasn't changing, just their understanding of it. Eventually people gave in and let the sun become the center of their universe. But that didn't last. Now, when we look out, it seems like we're in the center again. Galaxies are rushing away from us equally in all directions. But we know we're not in the center. There is no center."

Dad liked stringing sentences together, like a spider spinning a web.

"Hubble," he went on. "We see the galaxies rushing away, but into what? No telling. That's our reality. For now."

He took a sip of coffee.

"Have you noticed that every discovery makes us smaller? Reality only gets bigger. We're more and more a pinpoint all the time. Maybe one day we'll discover we don't even exist."

"Dad—"

"We're so insignificant, size-wise. How did Carl Sagan put it? Yes. We're a 'mote of dust suspended in a sunbeam'. What an image. Every creature that has ever lived and died has done so on a blue speck in a black void in a distant corner of a single galaxy. That's the truth, as far as we know. And we barely know anything."

He looked in my eyes like he was searching for truth.

"In Genesis, God says 'Let there be light.'"

"So I've heard."

"He makes the light on day one, then the sun on day four."

"Okay…so?"

Dad looked harder into my eyes, searching somewhere behind them.

"Where was the light on day one coming from if not from the sun? It's Earth's only light source."

"The Bible was written a long time ago. People were trying to make sense of the world. They didn't have much to work with."

"Not much to work with—funny."

Dad didn't laugh. He instead reached for his coffee.

"People love stories, Jax. We're made of them.

Stories are mirrors we hold up to the world, some beautiful, some ugly. Reflections can be surprising. I say this because—imagine for a minute what it's like to have a brain like mine. I see things you don't see—like Ms. Jakintsu. She may not be real to you, but she's part of my story. When you tell me she's not real, you sound crazy to me, like you're telling me there's no sun. It's hard to live someone else's truth."

* * *

As it turned out, Dad was right. I had to abandon my version of truth for Josh's.

Pronouns were tricky. *He*, *she*, *him*, *her*—these little words, once spoken on instinct, now had to be consciously chosen. When Josh was out to me and only me, I had to switch between male and female like a double agent. It figures I'd end up an English teacher.

"You should tell Mom." That was my advice. I wanted someone else to know. Carrying the knowledge by myself was a burden fit for Atlas. "Mom will get that you're still…you."

I was talking like Dad, understanding one reality and living another, doing my best to balance opposing worlds that both felt real.

"Mom could handle it—eventually," Josh said. "What about Dad?"

I pictured her sitting Dad down, having spent hours planning each and every word, only to say: Dad, from now on, don't call me Josh. Call me Angelica.

"I was talking with Dad," Angelica explained when I asked how she had chosen the new name. "It was just me and him and of course he starts talking about Ms. Jakintsu and how her garden's doing great this year, blah blah blah. At some point he tells me Ms. Jakintsu gave him something special, the ground-up roots of a plant called angelica. I forget the details—you know how Dad goes off. Anyway, he told me the angelica mixture was made especially for me."

"Why you?"

"Ms. Jakintsu said it would protect me against negative energy, so Dad sprinkled it around our house. He said—" Angelica smiled. "He said the angelica was a shield, that nothing in the world could hurt me...Lame, I know. But ever since then I've always liked the name Angelica. It was like, when I gave myself a new name, I felt real. I existed. And I have a shield against bad energy."

"Like a superhero."

"Anyway, I didn't name myself after Angelica from *Rugrats*, in case you were wondering."

It felt good to laugh.

"Honestly," she said, "what do you think Dad would say if I told him?"

Would Dad start seeing Angelica like he saw Ms. Jakintsu? His own child would risk joining the cast of figments in his imagination.

"Dad's just—he's not like other dads."

"I get it," Angelica cut in. "You think he'll be confused, freaked out."

I wanted to tell her she had already confused and freaked *me* out. But I was the only one she trusted, the only person on Earth who called her Angelica. To everyone else she was still Josh. I was her confidant. We were siblings, best friends, and my discomfort ran as deep as the roots of our family tree. I felt the unease in my bones. Primordial. My angst was like a cold I couldn't shake and for which there was no medicine.

I wanted so much to feel better, but on top of my angst was a visceral anger. My own brother had lied to me for years. Why hadn't Josh trusted me?

I wanted to go back in time and grow up again.

* * *

After a while, Angelica told me she was ready.

"I'm gonna tell them."

I froze.

"But—I mean, it's not that Dad couldn't handle…your thing." Had I just called the truth Angelica's *thing*? "Dad gets so confused. Like when they put up a Dunkin' Donuts where that park used to be. He was angry for weeks. That was Dad's park. He walked there every day. To him, when they closed it, I bet it felt like betrayal."

Angelica's face went pale. I had just equated her coming out with treason.

She picked the dead skin around her unpainted nail beds.

"You really think it'd be that hard for him?" she

asked, a glimmer of hope in her voice.

"Tell Mom. She'll have your back. And you know I do."

I wasn't sure if I did or if Mom would either. Angelica's half-hearted smile told me she already knew that.

I touched her shoulder, determined to stop venting my own feelings and focus on hers.

"Look. Forget what I said about the park and Dunkin' Donuts. It was stupid. You're right. You should tell them—both of them."

Angelica, an invisible minority, weighed the costs and benefits of becoming visible.

"Why not tell Mom today?" I pushed. "Right now. I'll go with you!"

"Okay, chill out, Jax."

"Seriously. Let's go!"

"Shut up. Someone will hear you."

"What the hell difference does it make *when* you tell?" I barked. "They're gonna find out sooner or later. Why not now?"

Angelica picked at her thumbnail.

"You love Mom's kosheri," she said. "You always have."

I was thrown by the mention of food.

"Yeah. So?"

"I love it too. Family tradition. But what if after all these years of Mom's cooking and watching you eat her kosheri you walked up to her out of the blue and told her you actually hate it? 'Hey Mom, guess what…?'

She'd look at you like you're crazy, probably cry."

Angelica sighed. The very fact that she was having to explain this to me was clearly exhausting.

"Then Mom would ask why you never said anything before. Why would you keep something like that a secret for so many years? Better yet, how *could* you? Now it's suddenly your fault and Mom's thinking: Oh my God…if he doesn't like kosheri then what else isn't he telling me? Who is this person?"

My heart was racing.

"Okay," Angelica laughed, "so Egyptian stew isn't the best comparison, but you see my point. Coming out means Mom will remember all those boys' clothes and boys' toys and boys' bathrooms—all the way back to the baby shower where she probably got a bunch of blue junk from her friends. She'll feel like she did something wrong, or that I resent her. And neither is true."

"That's why you have to tell her!"

"It's not that easy. If you were me, what would you say? What would you expect her to say back?"

I wiped beads of sweat from my forehead.

"I'll tell her when I'm ready," Angelica said. "Not tonight. But soon."

"Josh," I implored—starting to cry—and then, realizing I had used her birth name, corrected myself. "Angelica, why didn't you tell me sooner?" The question felt futile. "I wish I'd known. Why didn't you just tell me? Or anyone? I hate knowing you felt alone when I've been here all along. I feel like such an idiot."

Angelica laughed.

"Sorry," she said, covering her mouth. "I don't know why I laughed. It's not funny. You're not an idiot. But it was nice to hear you call yourself one."

* * *

She never used the kosheri metaphor with Mom. When the time came, Angelica spoke with actions, not words. She went back to that store and bought the red dress in the window—a dress to do the explaining. I'm not sure where she got the money.

The dress fell to the mannequin's ankles but dropped to the floor on thirteen-year-old Angelica. She put on lipstick and a pair of red heels too big for her feet, both swiped from Mom's closet. She looked like an underage drag queen.

Angelica had dressed in the bedroom we shared. Two twin beds, soccer ball wallpaper, light blue paint, a ceiling fan whirring overhead, and a poster of Buffy the Vampire Slayer on the wall. My comforter was patterned with soccer balls and music notes. Angelica's comforter was midnight blue with yellow Batman ovals.

"I'm ready," she said with a smile-for-the-camera grin.

Angelica looked like a boy in a dress. As she stood in the middle of our bedroom under the ceiling fan, a crazy question entered my mind—a strange, very Dad kind of question: *What is a boy?*

Josh had proven there was no such thing as "the obvious." There was body, then gender. They didn't always match. We both had Y-chromosomes. I felt male, Angelica didn't.

It looked weird because I wasn't used to it, but weird is different from wrong. Angelica had put on a dress. So what? It was weird, not wrong. No deity had appeared to smite her, no dark clouds or claps of thunder, no bolts of lightning hurled from the heavens. The fan in our bedroom kept spinning. The world kept turning.

I attempted a compliment.

"You look—"

My mind said Angelica; my eyes saw Josh.

"That bad, huh?" she laughed, hiking up the bottom of the dress. "I don't care how it looks. Just go get Mom so I can get this over with."

I went downstairs to the kitchen where Mom was finishing dinner, which was, as it was every Friday, her famous Egyptian stew. The kitchen was a bouquet of sautéed garlic and spicy tomato sauce. How could anyone hate kosheri?

"You okay, Jax?" she asked upon seeing me.

My stomach churned.

"Sweetie, you're all pale. You feeling sick?"

"No, no." I forced a smile. "Just hungry. When's dinner?"

"In—minutes—or—after—dessert."

I caught only snippets, too busy in my own head. I lingered in the kitchen, digging my hands deep into my pockets for an escape.

"You sure you're okay, Jax? You should sit down. Do you have a fever?"

She stared at me, eyes bulging with concern. She was picturing the scar beneath my hair where I had banged my skull on the bathroom floor.

"I'm fine."

She went back to stirring the sauce.

"Well, I'm glad you're hungry." She closed her eyes and leaned over the steaming pot of lentils for a whiff. "Good batch. Rice is just about done."

"Yeah. Rice. Oh—before I forget," I tried to add casually, "Josh wants to talk to you."

"Where is he?"

"Who?"

"Josh."

"Oh—sh—er—he's upstairs. In our room."

Mom eyed me suspiciously.

"What's going on?"

Her stare doubled my heart rate.

"Josh is fine," I said. "He just asked me to tell you to go see him."

It felt weird to say *he* and *him*. Maybe after today we could end the pronoun war.

Mom took the wooden spoon out of the sauce for a lick.

"I'll just turn this off. Grab your father and get the table ready."

She walked by me, ran a hand through my hair, and went upstairs.

Dad was sitting on the couch with the TV off, not reading or sleeping, just sitting—normal behavior for him. The ticking of a clock, the muted sound of a distant car alarm, the pitter-patter of rain on the roof, the hum of clothes tumbling in the dryer—Dad's ears focused on noises that most people could tune out.

I sat down next to him.

"Something big," he muttered suddenly. "Very big."

"What did you say?"

He picked up the cup of coffee next to his chair and took a long sip.

"Something big is coming," he said, fixing his eyes across the room. "Big and soon."

I spoke through my surprise.

"How do you know?"

I wished he would look at me.

"You promise not to tell your mother?"

Time to pull back the curtain for another peek into his world.

"I promise."

"Ms. Jakintsu told me."

He seemed excited, like he was bursting at the seams with secrets.

"Dad," I started, cautious. I was about to reconfigure his reality for the umpteenth time. "You've talked about Ms. Jakintsu before. I know she's real to you, but she's not real to us. Do you remember?"

Dad looked at me, crushed. I hated being the one to remind him.

"Right. Yes. Of course." His face was cherry red. "Don't tell your mother I mentioned Ms. Jakin—Just forget I ever said anything. Please."

He stared into the darkness.

I wondered how Mom and Angelica were doing upstairs. What had Mom's first words been when she opened the bedroom door? *Why the hell are you wearing my shoes?*

"Let's go set the table," I said to Dad. "It's kosheri night."

We went to the kitchen and filled our bowls. Mom was still upstairs, meeting her daughter. Dad was quiet. Ms. Jakintsu was on his mind.

"Okay," I started between bites. "We agree she's not real. Now tell me about your conversation. You said something big is coming?"

Why is there an obligation to discuss reality? The weather is boring; the news is depressing. You might as well enjoy what you discuss at dinner.

"We met this morning," Dad said, looking over his shoulder to see if the coast was clear.

"Where?"

"Her kitchen."

That was the usual spot.

"She's just back from a trip to Mexico," Dad went on. "She brought back a beautiful souvenir of a spotted dragon man with these little finger extensions that shoot off the sides. It looks like a Christian cross from a distance—brilliant, stunning colors. And—what was I saying? Oh, right. Like I said, Jax, big changes are coming. That's what she told me. Brace yourself."

Changes. For all I knew he could have been at the supermarket this morning when that David Bowie song came on. His brain heard the words and his visual cortex turned the supermarket into Ms. Jakintsu's kitchen. And maybe there was someone in line at the checkout with a spotted dragon figurine, or a tarnished speckled cross that looked dragon-like at a distance, or maybe a tattoo of a dragon, or of Mexico. No telling. Dad's brain could whisk him away anytime, anywhere, and Ms. Jakintsu's kitchen was where he usually went.

"About these changes that are coming," I said. "Can you be more specific?"

He scratched his chin.

"Ms. Jakintsu only said that for once, everyone's reality would change, not just mine."

CHAPTER THREE

What's uglier than red?

The longer I stare at Angelica's fingernails, the more they upset me. There's already too much red in the world—the color of gore and scars, of conquest and torches, forbidden fruit, ink on failed tests, embarrassment, rust, rage, emergency lights—the tangle of red tape at hospitals, clipboards of tiny print detailing what's not covered by insurance—the fear of red cards, red meat, being in the red, being caught red-handed. Red is the color of heartbreak, spilled wine, murder and revenge. Red is the color of the stitched-up wounds across my sister's face.

Mom's eyes are bloodshot.

"What did the doctor say?" I ask.

I clutch at hope, a feeling that, in the ICU, is colorless. I stare into Mom's tired Egyptian face. Her shoulders slouch under the weight of grief and gravity. Her hair is a bramble of grey and black split ends.

"Mom? What did the doctor say?"

"The coffee."

"What?"

"So bad. Vending machine. Only thing to eat. You have anything? Granola bar? Gum? Sugar, I could use. Lifesaver?"

Her syntax was unraveling.

"There's not a cafeteria?"

"I did have one of those square crumbly things filled with goo you kids loved to eat growing up."

"Pop-Tarts?"

Every now and then she reminds me she was raised by immigrants.

"Pop-Tarts. Funny name. Because they pop. Out of the toaster."

"Mom, what did the doctor tell you?"

"You know how they are. They keep things vague. Afraid you'll turn around and sue if they're wrong. Can't be wrong if they're too vague to be understood. Play it safe."

"The doctor didn't say—never mind. Just tell me what they told you."

Mom can be harder to talk to than Dad.

"I thought I understood English, but these words: unstable, serious, critical...I graduated from Yale and have no idea what they're saying."

"They said Angelica's in critical condition?"

"I'd thought critical meant serious but not life-threatening, which is what I remember them telling me at some point, though who knows if I'm remembering it right. Apparently that's what the word critical means in some hospitals—but jargon being jargon, it varies from place to place. Like pizza."

"Mom, please."

"What does 'pizza' even mean, at its most basic?" Mom raises her index and middle fingers to make air quotes around *pizza*. "It's different to everyone. Triangular, square, red sauce, white sauce, thin crust, thick, New York style, deep dish…Who's to say what pizza really is?"

She again puts air quotes around 'pizza', using abstraction to avoid reality.

"Mom. Angelica."

She glances at the body on the bed.

"I've heard far too many words today. I feel like an immigrant in one of your ESL classes. I feel like my mother."

"Jesus, Mom. *Stop.*"

She looks at her feet and kicks the floor, leaving a scuffmark. Then she looks over at the bed.

"They—some people—a group of guys— men—by the cemetery—on Grove Street. They *did* this to her. They dragged her into the cemetery and did this to her." Mom motions without looking toward Angelica's patchwork of bloody stitches. "It happened on her way home from work. You know she works late at the restaurant on Tuesdays."

Mom wipes her leaky red eyes.

"I left your father at home," she says, anticipating my next question. "I told him I was going out to do some errands and wouldn't be back for a while."

"He doesn't know? We can't just leave him. If Angelica's in critical condition—"

"She'll be *fine*," Mom insists, as if stressing the last word will make it true. "Let's wait until Angelica's awake. Then we'll tell your dad to come."

The sight of Angelica's bloody face and swollen

eyes, the sound of machines beeping—I have to get out of here.

"I'm going to the house," I say. "And I'm coming back here with Dad."

Mom opens her mouth, inhales as if preparing for a longwinded argument, then nods.

Angelica lies still amidst the churning motors and beeping machines keeping her alive. Her face is Halloween-ready, a mishmash of wounds and clots.

My fists clench as I walk out of the room. Who were these men that hurt her?

* * *

When I was nine we went trick-or-treating. It was the Halloween after I had split my head open on the bathroom floor. Angelica, still going by Josh, was dressed as a blood-spattered Carrie. I was the clown from *It*.

While Mom did my makeup, I remember sitting on the toilet, which faced Angelica's favorite painting: Manet's *Argenteuil*.

Mom had picked it up at a yard sale as a touch-up for the bathroom, something to look at while people did their business. But to my sister, it was much more than a colorful print in a cheap wooden frame. Because of that painting, Angelica grew to love the distorted realities of French Impressionism at an early age. Like Dad's brain, Manet's work challenged reality. And his *Argenteuil* gave Angelica an excuse to pee sitting down.

"There's just something about the bright water and dark sky," Angelica told me. "It's the woman in the painting, the way she looks at you. It's all in her eyes, and her smile—not a big smile, just the hint of a smile. And not coy like the Mona Lisa's, but knowing, in control, like she's got something up her sleeve and you're about to find out what it is."

CHAPTER FOUR

I speed through downtown New Haven, racing through yellow lights across the nine squares of an Englishman's attempted utopia—a vibrant cluster of churches, banks, and municipal buildings, including the library where Mom and Dad would take me and Angelica every Sunday after breakfast.

Dad peeks out the living room window as I pull in the driveway. He comes outside to greet me. I haven't planned how to break the news.

He speaks first.

"I thought you'd come."

Mom must have called. He spreads his arms and starts toward me. I flinch. He hugs me, squeezing hard. Dad rarely hugs. When we part, he's crying. Then I start crying. We hug again, this time for ten full seconds. It's got to be a record for us.

"We need to go to the hospital," I say, choosing to be blunt. "Angelica's been hurt."

"It wasn't an accident." He looks down in anger. "Someone hurt her. On purpose."

I look to see if the neighbors are out, lowering my voice.

"Who told you that? Did Mom call?"

Dad looks left then right.

"Before I went to bed last night I was contacted." He steps closer and speaks low. "Ms.

Jakintsu told me something bad was coming."

I exhale in frustration, sighing like Mom.

"Now wait a minute," he says, grabbing me by the shoulders. "You think Ms. Jakintsu isn't real. I know that. But what if you let her be real, for my sake, just for today."

"Why today?"

"Ms. Jakintsu may be able to help Angelica. And time is short."

I decide without thinking.

"Fine. Take me to her." Dad is visibly shocked. "Where is she? Does she still live in East Rock like she did when I was young?"

Over two decades' worth of Jakintsu stories resurface in my mind.

"Yes," Dad says. "Same house, right here in the neighborhood."

No use trying to coax him back to reality. I need to get us to the hospital. But Angelica's face, those stitches...there's time for a detour.

"It's nearby?"

"What?"

"Ms. Jakintsu's place. It's close?"

"Yes. Sorry. I'm not used to hearing you talk about her."

"Let's go."

"Jax, wait." He grabs my arm as I turn to leave. "You're sure about this? If you're going to do this, you need to take it seriously."

I yank my arm out of his grasp.

"I want to meet her," I say. "But if she's not there, we'll go straight to the hospital. Deal?"

It might be easier for him to face Angelica once he gets Ms. Jakintsu out of his mind. It's not enough for me to say there's no woman named Ms. Jakintsu, not today. I've been telling him that since I was a kid. Everyone has.

I don't have the energy for a tug of war over what's real and what's not.

"We'll take my car," I say, attempting an even tone through my impatience.

"I hope she's there," Dad says. No one likes to be proven wrong. "Our visits are usually planned. I don't just drop in whenever I feel like it. She invites me. She sees many people, Jax. She might be busy with a client."

On another day I might have laughed.

"Witchcraft is her business then?"

"More advice-giving than witchcraft. But yes. It's a sort of business, though she's never charged me."

"So she's an oracle?"

"That's Greek mythology."

"And the Matrix."

I put the car in reverse and whip out of the driveway, half paying attention to the road, and half to Dad.

"I liked that movie," Dad says. "But life isn't The Matrix. You don't get to choose what pill you swallow. You're born with the genes you get, with however much or little money your parents have to raise you with. It's like Hindus say: life is a web. The thread we get to make our web is a product of birth. In other words, chance. Circumstance. Only people of fortunate birth believe in fate. Fate is a luxurious idea. It's easy to believe in fate when you're born into nice circumstances. When your obstacles feel surmountable. When your future feels beautiful and certain, like tomorrow's sunrise. But what about the others? The ones who are dirt poor and go to bed hungry? The ones whose parents beat them? The ones whose societies discriminate against them? The ones whose genes cause them to die young? The ones who would have lived if only vaccines were affordable? People don't start on equal footing in life—not socially, not genetically. We don't choose where or when, or even *what* we are. We're just born, without our consent, and we have to make the most of it."

He pauses.

"What was I talking about before?"

"The Matrix?"

"After that."

"Something about a web?"

"Yes!" He scratches his chin. "Sorry, Jax. I don't remember what my point was. Forget it."

"Just answer me plainly," I say, stepping on the gas. "Who is Ms. Jakintsu?"

Dad has been told and retold since his late twenties that what he sees and hears may be fictional, a byproduct of unhealthy neuro-circuitry that doctors don't fully understand. Besides his occasional hallucinations, he is an otherwise healthy man.

Still, after all these years, I search for explanations, look for logic in the madness, demand reason knowing there is none.

"Ms. Jakintsu is a woman with special abilities," Dad says. "It's not complicated."

"She's magical?"

"Magic is available to anyone gifted enough to harness and use it."

"Can you define magic?"

"It's not something you're born with, or something you can see, like lightning bolts shooting out your fingertips. Ms. Jakintsu is not a Halloween witch. No pointy black hat, no broom—though, come to think of it, she does have a cat…Turn left up here."

We pass the markets on Orange Street and head toward the woods.

"Is she a Pagan?" I press. "Ceremonies at the solstice? That sort of thing?"

"She knows a few Pagans in the Linguistics Department at Yale. I also know one who teaches a class on Old English. Lovely lady. But Ms. Jakintsu doesn't belong to a coven. She operates alone."

"What exactly are these 'special abilities' that she has?"

I hear myself getting argumentative.

"She believes that the body is a vehicle for the soul."

"Most religions do."

"I suppose so."

"What's a soul, according to her?"

All his answers beg for questions.

"Soul is not good or evil. Those are human words. Soul isn't just human. It's animal, rock, river, cloud—soul is nature's fabric. One soul we share. A giant web. Or better yet, a pie. And we've all got an equal slice."

"One soul for all of us?"

"Our soul is the sum of an equation too big for any one of us to see. We live together, breathe together. When we die, we rot and become plants that give off oxygen. Our bodies become soil. Wind and rivers shape the soil. We are the wind, and we are the riverbanks. Our flesh and blood turn into flowers. Flowers bear fruit. We eat the fruit. And we are the fruit."

"So, according to Ms. Jakintsu, fruit eaters are cannibals?"

He laughs.

"With quite a few very comfortable degrees of separation. In the same way your third cousin twice removed is technically related to you."

"Is Ms. Jakintsu a Buddhist? What you said was pretty Zen."

He stops to think.

"She says sometimes people get lost in the life cycle, thrown off course. Pushed aside. Ms. Jakintsu can communicate with those who've been lost, the ones that have been disconnected—like a single bead severed from a necklace. She can find the lost bead and help it reconnect to the necklace. That's her special ability, and her business."

"Then she's a medium. She talks to ghosts?"

I want him to define his abstraction.

"Ms. Jakintsu helps people reconnect with things they've lost—even themselves. Some people are stuck. They feel outside. They want to get back."

"Back to what?"

"They've been severed, kicked out...Take a left at the intersection. The point is, Jax, you can't understand what the lost bead feels like if you've always been attached to the necklace."

The car moves over patched-up potholes down a forgotten side street of old Victorians. Dad sucks in a nervous breath.

"You can park anywhere on this side," he directs with a pointed finger. "Her house is that big old yellow one up there behind the hedge."

The house sits up beyond the sidewalk on a grassy knoll between two other houses much like it. The dull yellow paint chips and curls off the sides. Black shingles on the roof are speckled with patches of green moss. The house's tall windows are shielded by shutters. Perched atop the second floor is a rectangular widow's watch with a tiny witch-hat roof. The whole house emits an unhurried air of classy decay, like the British monarchy.

No black cats cross our path. No crows caw from telephone wires.

Dad starts toward the driveway with a bounce in his step. Whatever hesitation he had felt in the car is gone, now transferred to me.

"Coming, Jax?"

I should never have played into his delusion. What was I thinking? Angelica is in the hospital. Mom is waiting for us. This is absurd.

I take out my phone and start dialing. Then I imagine how it will sound: Hi, Mom. Dad and I are making a pit stop at Ms. Jakintsu's. Be there soon!

I pocket the phone and lock the car doors. No traffic but a few crisscrossing birds in this sleepy part of New Haven.

"Doesn't look like she's home," I attempt.

"We haven't even knocked. Come on!"

We're really going through with it. I hope the disappointment won't crush him, and that some maniac Boo Radley type doesn't come barreling out the door with a shotgun.

We walk past the hedge up the driveway to the back of the house. The backyard is a square plot of land big enough for a dog to bury a bone in. Tomato plants and herbs grow alongside the house.

Dad walks up the steps to the door and raises a clenched fist to knock.

"Don't!" my voice yells on instinct.

"What? Why not?"

"I'm sorry I brought us here. Let's just go."

After all, this has to be someone's house.

"But Jax—you said you wanted to come." His look of bewilderment is an arrow through my heart. I've confused him. "Why did we drive here if you don't want to meet her?"

A part of me has always been curious to see the big old house and its kitchen built for secret conversations, the place Dad escapes to in his mind.

Yes. Who cares? Let him knock. Let us both confront our delusions.

As soon as he puts his hand up again, the knob jiggles and the door opens. An old woman with sunbaked skin and bushy eyebrows appears.

"Hello, Kyle. I thought you will be coming today." The woman speaks with an accent I can't pinpoint. "I already cut bread for spicy snack. Good weather today for spicy."

The woman wears a red wool sweater and blue jeans. Wrapped over her hair is a blue paisley pattern kerchief. From her ears dangle large golden hoop earrings.

Something rings in her pocket. She pulls out a smartphone and puts it to her ear. She starts speaking rapidly in a language I don't understand. Then she hangs up, slides her finger across the touch screen, and types something out.

"I just changing one appointment for my calendar. Okay, I finish."

She pockets the phone.

"Are you sure we're not bothering you?" Dad asks. "Our visit is unplanned. My son wanted to meet you and I thought we'd stop by."

"No bother. Come in. We have big work today. Life no always give us room for appointment."

She turns her gaze to me, eyes small and warm, the color of chestnuts. One eye seems to look *at* me and the other *through* me. Her lips are pursed into the hint of a smile, as if she's thinking of a joke she doesn't want to share. And yet something about her seems wary, a little off kilter, ever so slightly berserk. A bit of black hair pokes out from beneath her kerchief.

I stand rigid in the driveway, straddling the border between worlds.

"Jax, dear boy," she says with a croak. "My name is Ms. Jakintsu."

She looks at me longer than comfort allows, eying me from head to toe like a tailor would a client.

"Poor boy, he is have shock," she tells my father with a sympathetic smile. "No is easy when fiction become fact so suddenly. You must to change your thinking. Oh well. This, we call life! Now come inside. We have big work to do."

CHAPTER FIVE

Her kitchen is an ecosystem. As drab as the house looked from outside, the inside swells with color, and with the smell of seafood baking. Goldenrod walls support tall cupboards standing proud like redwoods. Chiseled log beams tied off at the ends by thick ropes bridge the wood-slat ceiling. Hung across the golden walls are dozens of ceramic and cast iron plates, all painted with exotic flora and fauna. Each plate hangs peacefully on its nail, keeping to its spot on the wall, pleased with the balance of power in the room.

In the center of the kitchen is a wooden table with three chairs, three cups, three spoons, and a hot teakettle—as if she had been expecting us.

The old woman's back curls like a seahorse's tail.

"You like?"

She points to something on the countertop. Overhead kitchen light shines down on the object: a carving of a casserole dish with a wooden turkey inside. Like the rest of the kitchen, the colors on the dish are warm and vibrant, a careful smear of yellows and reds with a splash of orange on the head. Painted onto the beak is a black line curved up into a smile—the hint of a smile, like Ms. Jakintsu's.

"This is *alebrije* from San Martín Tilcajete," she tells my father. "You like?"

"Very much. But my favorite is still the spotted dragon man—the one you found in Oaxaca de Juárez all those years ago." Dad pronounces the name with a good accent. When did he pick up Spanish? "I see the dragon man's not in his spot near the sink. Did you trade him for the turkey?"

"I will never trade spotted dragon man," Ms. Jakintsu says, half smiling. "I know what he mean to you. He moved to living room, change scenery. Plates move twice every year. Everything need new perspective or our thoughts become lazy. But this one..." She points to the turkey in the casserole dish. "Vendor who sell me it call it *el guajolote sereno*. She was insist that I buy. I want to ask why but I no could speak her language."

"Zapotec?"

"Yes. From sixty Zapotec language, I speak only two. No was language of this woman. Bad luck! I ask her to sing something in her language. Music no need words, so beautiful. After I buy, she say me to have safe way back to America. You can believe this? She think I was American!"

"You've assimilated!" Dad says, laughing and fake-stamping an invisible passport. "Next stop: citizenship!"

"I study for test," the old woman says. "But I never remember what year those men—how you say? Your Starting Fathers? I no remember when they write your Constitution. 1785?"

I slip into the conversation.

"So you're from Oaxaca then?"

Her accent could be Spanish, though it doesn't sound like the accents of my Spanish-speaking students.

"No, no am from Oaxaca."

"But you're from Mexico?"

Ms. Jakintsu unties her kerchief then rewraps it tightly around her hair.

"Why this worry for where people from?"

She frowns and shuffles toward the oven. Then she turns to address me again.

"My accent is many years of travel, many language, much time and life. I apologize. My English is more and more bad. More I grow old, more I forget rules, mix grammars of many language. You know, my first language, this one is impossible to learn. In English you have big vocabulary, many words for one idea, but in my language we use only one word for one idea, like *iparsortalderatu*, which is mean you should walk north. Crazy to learn grammar for my language. Because this reason, government make us learn Spanish in school."

She opens the oven, bends over, and looks inside.

Dad eyes me and nods toward Ms. Jakintsu, a sign to keep talking. I scan the room for a new topic. My eyes land on the edge of the countertop where there stands a clear container filled with gritty black stuff.

"What's in that, over there on the counter?—if you don't mind my asking."

The old woman glances at the container, then looks away. Slipping on a pair of oven mitts, she pulls a steaming tray of baked mussels from the oven. She whiffs and smiles, inspecting the tray with her chestnut eyes to fish out the few mussels whose shells never opened.

"Eat snack while txipirones finish to cook."

It's early for lunch but the aroma has me salivating. Ms. Jakintsu takes a mussel, tips back her head, and slurps it down.

"Is sand," she says, wiping her mouth. She glances toward the container I had asked about. "Black sand. Is familiar to you, no?"

Is this why Dad thinks she's magical? Black sand and cryptic comments? She's probably only mysterious because her grammar is bad. Adds to the mystique.

"My home is on mouth of river," she says. "The river put black sand on our beach, no is unhealthy like your capitalist oil sand. Mine is black color by nature."

Dad turns to me.

"Beautiful, isn't it?"

She continues explaining herself.

"I was born in bathtub in old city neighborhood. Our house was white like chalk, small red roof, red like blood from cow. My father was fisherman, like his father and grandfather. They hunt whales in past time, but no more. My father loved to tell stories, just like your father."

She smiles at Dad as if she has known him forever. Then she continues.

"My mother was strong. Three hours before I

was born she was in forest cutting logs on my ceiling. Later, when no money was coming and land was dry, she went for work in city factory making soup cans. Now those jobs and my mother are gone. Factory now is company for—how you say Spanish word *cirugía*?"

Dad wipes mussel juice from his mouth.

"Surgery."

"Company is make tools for sur—surge—for this crazy English word you say."

She ponders my plate of mussels.

"Eat, Jax," she prods like a grandmother. "You need much strength today."

Dad has already downed four mussels and reaches for a fifth. I take one, crack the steaming shell, and let the warm buttery brine trickle down my throat.

"Where exactly did you say you were born?" I ask.

"My house, bathtub."

"I mean—what city?"

"Mutriku. Spanish say 'Motrico'. People who come from over mountains—people with money—they call it *pays basque*. Some visit for to make—how you say—*erromeria*, we call it in my language. Spanish say *peregrinación*, long travel. What is called in English?"

Dad shrugs.

"You know people who going on *camino de Santiago*, road for Galicia?"

"The Route to Santiago de Compostela, you mean?"

"Yes."

"Pilgrimage."

"What you say?"

"It's the word you were looking for," Dad tells her. "People who take the pilgrimage to see Saint James. You were saying they pass through your hometown on their way."

"Yes. In French, James they call him *Saint Jacques*, and my cousin who live in Lapurdi, she tell me that scallop, they call it *coquilles Saint-Jacques*. Funny, no? She say road lines on map to Galicia look like scallop shell lines, all go to same place."

"Makes sense."

Their ability to understand each other is stunning.

"These days," the old woman goes on, "people coming less for pilgrim— for pilgrim—"

"Pilgrimage."

"Less this and more business, speaking Spanish, French, *alemán*. And all speak English—beautiful English, like me! Jax, you help people to speak this English, is your job, no?"

"Yes, that's right." I put down a mussel shell. "So you're from Spain then?"

Wrinkles multiply on her face as she holds a steady half smile.

"I just explain you who am I and where do I come from."

She looks back at the container of black sand on the countertop.

"That is me, from sand. And my beach I think

47

you already visit, long time ago, by accident. When you hit your head in bathroom, no?"

The tucked-away memory is instantly awakened, electrical signals zapping a sleepy clump of neural mesh in my brain. I had completely forgotten about the beach. Dad had called it Ms. Jakintsu's beach. Was he now remembering too?

Ms. Jakintsu gazes at me like one might a sunset. Something rubs up against my right shin under the table, causing me to leap up in shock.

Dad chuckles.

"It's only Katu."

"He like you!" Ms. Jakintsu says.

Katu, with fur the color of dusk, is rotund. The basement of this old house must be teeming with mice. The cat sits and purrs, its tail swooping back and forth across the floor. The animal inspects me with emerald eyes.

It dawns on me: I'm in a woman's house—a real woman—whose name is Ms. Jakintsu, and who, in my father's mind, is some kind of guru who does *pro bono* work with the spirit world and makes delicious appetizers.

So what? Dad's got a kooky old immigrant friend. No harm in that. At least he hasn't been paying her. Still, it was foolish to come inside. We should go to the hospital and face reality.

"Thank you for the mussels, ma'am, but I'm afraid we can't stay."

Dad frowns.

"What's wrong, Jax?"

Ms. Jakintsu bows her head humbly.

"Your son no is comfortable. I say too much too fast, is my fault. I talk and no listen, this is my weakness. Now I listen. You talk."

"We don't have *time* to talk," I say in a voice louder than necessary. "Look, Ms. Jakin—ma'am. Whoever you are. Please. There's been an emergency. Family crisis. Obviously you and my dad know each other. I'm surprised, I admit. Very surprised, but—"

"He no mention me before?"

"No, he has. Many times. I'm just surprised."

"Surprise for what?"

"I'm surprised that you're, well—"

"Real?"

I hate that she said it. I wanted my sentence to dangle unfinished. Of course you're real, you old crone!

"Look," I say. "Maybe you already know this but my father, he sometimes sees and hears things. I'll be honest. I thought you were—well, I guess I thought you might be a character from one of his many stories. But I see now you're obviously not. I'm sorry. It's taking me a minute to process the fact that you've actually been here this whole time."

Or maybe she hasn't. Maybe Dad has been visiting multiple women and calling them all Ms. Jakintsu.

Whatever the case, we shouldn't have brushed him off so quickly when he tried to talk about her. We should have followed him here years ago. When did he find the time to visit? How had he slipped in and out of the house unnoticed so many times, and for so many years? How could Mom, Angelica, and I have been so dismissive?

The old woman's forehead folds with concern.

"Why you are angry?"

"We can't stay right now," I tell her. "Someday, another time, I'd love to come back and get to know you. You obviously mean a lot to my dad. But right now we have to get to the hospital."

Ms. Jakintsu stands up and slips on her oven mitts again. When she opens the oven, a warm breeze of fragrant air escapes once more into the kitchen. This time she removes a sizzling casserole dish.

"Nothing to do in hospital," she says vaguely, bringing the hot dish to the table. "Your sister already go to another place, safe place for waiting."

"What? Who are you talking about?"

"Angelica, of course."

Mad logic, just like Dad. Unreal. Surreal. This house, this kitchen, these colorful hanging plates—are they moving, dancing? Is the Zapotec turkey figurine smiling at me?

"What do *you* know about Angelica?" I ask.

She looks me square in the eye, visibly offended that I would ask such a question.

"Many things in life I know, and many things in life are mystery. But Angelica, this, I know well."

"You've met her before?"

"No."

"Then how do you know her?"

"I know her like I know you, from so many stories of your father."

Who does this woman think she is? She's gone from a nice old foreigner to a condescending Yoda impersonator.

My mouth opens and words rush out faster than I can think.

"Of course you know us! You know *all* of us. You're Ms. Jakintsu, wise witch of New Haven, Connecticut! Not exactly how I'd pictured, with your blue jeans and smartphone, but at least you've got the drafty old house and a creepy cat."

"Jax, calm down," Dad says. "You're being rude. You asked to come here, remember? I know it's hard for you to accept, but this is my reality. I let you in. You agreed to accept it—just for today."

"Stop it, Dad. This house, this woman." I jab an accusatory index finger in Ms. Jakintsu's direction.

The two of them stare, waiting for me to continue. I pant like a sprinter nearing a finish line but find nothing else to say.

"Is true your father has sickness in his brain," Ms. Jakintsu says. "He can see and hear invisible thing. Brain chemical for him are different from healthy people. But this no is important today."

"Not important?" I ask.

"No is focus for today," she says. "We have other work together. No matter what is real for you, for him, for me. We discuss Angelica now. She is real for all of us. And she need our help."

Ms. Jakintsu bores her chestnut eyes into mine.

"Listen," she implores as if I weren't already. "Some people no like that Angelica is real. They become angry because she is real. They hate this reality. They want to change it. So they make violence to get Angelica out. You understand?"

Tears well up as I reach into my pocket.

"I need...I'm sorry, I need to call my mom."

I barely make out the screen through a watery blur. One ring. Two.

"Hello? Jax? Are you with your dad?"

"Yes," I say, soothed by the sound of her voice. "I picked him up at home. We ended up going to— we're just stopping for a minute to put gas in the—"

"Jax," she interrupts. "Don't come to the hospital. Not right now."

A distant-sounding sniffle. Mom has moved the phone away from her face. I picture the vacant hospital walls. I smell the chemicals of cleanliness and death.

Over the line, Mom breathes in to speak. My muscles tense up. Paralysis. I feel like I did on that beach of black sand—on Ms. Jakintsu's beach.

I hold my breath to stop time, or for good luck, like Angelica and I used to do in the backseat when Dad would drive through tunnels.

Mom sniffs again.

"Angelica's in a coma."

CHAPTER SIX

"The txipirones are excellent!" Dad says after a bite of blackened rice.

"This is recipe of my father."

The cat rubs up against my legs under the table.

"Katu, come here," the old woman says.

The cat ogles me under Ms. Jakintsu's gentle caress.

"That was Mom," I say to the room, pocketing my phone. "Angelica…she's in a coma."

"That's what Ms. Jakintsu was trying to tell us before you went on a tirade," Dad says, not the least bit surprised by the news. "Angelica's already gone to another place, a safe place. Weren't you listening?"

Dad is making things up, filling in gaps, drawing conclusions, grasping at straws.

"Come on, Dad. It's time for us to go home."

Ms. Jakintsu turns to him.

"Kyle, you never tell Jax about when you first know Angelica?"

Dad smiles.

"No, I don't think so."

I hate that they share memories.

"You mean when Josh came out?" I ask.

"Before that," the old woman says, adjusting her kerchief. "Tell him, Kyle. Is nice, this story."

"It was Halloween," Dad starts before I can

stop him. "Jax, you were nine or ten. It was just after you'd fallen in the bathroom."

I glance again at the jar of black sand. He remembers the fall. Does he remember the beach?

"You and Angelica went trick-or-treating as Stephen King characters that year. You were dressed as that ridiculous clown. What's his name? The one Tim Curry played."

"Pennywise, from *It*."

"Yes, that's right. And Josh—Angelica—was dressed as Carrie on prom night." I look at Ms. Jakintsu, who nods along knowingly as she pets her fat orange cat. "Before we went out for candy, Josh gave me a really big hug. And you know I'm not—I don't usually hug. It was just something about Josh that night, so comfortable with himself in that costume, so happy to be going out in disguise. It felt like, well, it felt special. I can't say it was the moment I realized I had a daughter. I never had a moment like that per se. It just felt very special, like I was seeing Josh in a way I hadn't before, more candid, more himself. Anyway, that Halloween hug is a memory I am proud to say I have never misplaced in my messy brain."

I think back to how I tried to talk Josh out of telling Dad. He's too fragile, I had said, too unstable, unpredictable. Those adjectives were all for me.

"You've always been astute," I say.

"Perhaps," Dad says. "But I don't presume to know what's real. No one else presumes I do either."

"Well you were right about Angelica, and about

Ms. Jakintsu," I admit, looking at the old woman. "Here she is, flesh and bones."

She turns a pair of chestnut eyes on me.

"You think I have bones?"

My neck tingles as I jolt upright.

"You…don't?"

She covers her mouth to cackle.

"Joke, my dear! You have too much stress."

"I just found out my sister's in a coma, so yes, I'm stressed."

"Of course," she says. "Tell me another story."

"A story?" I ask, caught off guard. "About what?"

"Angelica."

She rises and walks toward the container of black sand.

"You mean when we were kids?"

"Yes."

She brings the container to the table and opens the lid.

"Dad, are you sure you don't want to go home? We can leave."

He puts his hand over mine.

"Let yourself be here with me. Please."

Mom said not to go to the hospital. There's nothing else to do but wait. I turn to Ms. Jakintsu.

"You want to hear a story?"

"Very much."

"One Thanksgiving comes to mind from many years ago."

"You know I like turkey—like real American!"

The cat cranks its neck leftward to eyeball the colorful Zapotec souvenir.

"A family member came for dinner that year," I start. "My aunt from Ohio."

"Aunt Arwa?"

"How do you know—never mind. Yes, my Aunt Arwa. She usually comes for Thanksgiving."

Ms. Jakintsu stares, half smiling and expectant. Katu jumps on my lap and purrs. Dad looks at me and waits. Can this be real? My sister is in a coma and I'm here, relaxing, shooting the breeze, rehashing old times in a stranger's kitchen.

"It was high school," I say cautiously. "Freshman year. Word of Josh's coming out had leaked to both sides of the family."

Looking at Dad, I see there is nothing to be cautious about. After all these years, I'm still tiptoeing for nothing, still walking on eggshells I have strewn across my own path.

"There was a huge snow storm that year, but Aunt Arwa still made it for dinner…"

* * *

Twelve pounds of baked bird was far too much for five. We had expected ten at the table. The storm had stopped all in the family but Aunt Arwa, whose plane had landed just before snow took over the skies.

Mom and Dad sat at opposite ends of the table,

leaving Angelica on one side and me and Aunt Arwa on the other. Whipping wind rattled the bare trees beyond the window. We were thankful to be inside.

The conversation jumped from this to that, from how moist the turkey was to how scary the world was getting. It took a turn for the more personal as I reached for the stuffing.

"I'd like to speak openly, if I may," my aunt said. The time for small talk had come to an end. She was looking at Angelica. "Your mom told me that when you wear girls' clothes to school, you sometimes feel embarrassed."

Mom put up her hand like a traffic cop.

"Arwa, could you please not? We're trying to have dinner in peace."

"It's okay, Mom," Angelica said. "I don't mind."

Mom looked at Dad, then at Angelica. She gave a begrudging nod and a heavy sigh.

"Wearing the clothes isn't what's embarrassing," Angelica explained. "It's when people stare. It's embarrassing to be stared at."

Aunt Arwa shook her head.

"What worries me is it only takes a few blockheads to cause harm."

"My friends have my back," Angelica said. "And you guys, of course."

"I admire your courage," our aunt said. "But I must say, I'm baffled by all this. By your, well, the whole transformation. I just never thought—I never imagined a person could feel that way. Look. I know you're not the first person to do this. I've heard of it before. But do you think it could be at all influenced by culture?"

Angelica looked confused.

"What I mean is," our aunt went on, "it seems to be an especially Western thing, doesn't it?"

Mom slammed her fist on the table.

"What does *that* mean?"

"It means exactly what I said," Arwa answered, careful not to match her sister in tone. "I told you already. I want to speak openly about this. Not rudely, just openly. And what I'm saying is yes, I've heard of this kind of thing on the news—here, in *this* country."

"You think there are no transgender people in Egypt?" Mom asked.

"If there are I've certainly never heard of them."

"Maybe that's because people are too afraid to come out in Egypt. It's not the most welcoming place. As you might recall, our parents left for precisely that reason."

Aunt Arwa speared a piece of turkey and dipped it in gravy. She turned away from Mom to speak directly to Angelica.

"Just tell me, honey. Are you sure this is who you want to be?"

"It's who I already am."

"Yes, of course, but it's a big change. Physically. Will you start taking drugs to change your body? It could be dangerous and irreversible." Aunt Arwa paused to think out the wording of her next question. "How long have you known this is who you truly are?"

"Don't answer that," Mom jumped in.

"Seriously, Mom," Angelica said. "It's fine. Aunt Arwa is trying to understand."

"It's *not* fine," Mom fired back. "You shouldn't feel like you have to answer everybody's questions about your body. Your body is your business."

Aunt Arwa and Mom glared at each other. I admired the two for their strong convictions. Their sisterly sparring was part and parcel to our annual Thanksgiving feast, and honestly, something to look forward to.

When they took to arguing about the old days, they would often slip into Arabic. They could go on for a whole minute or two in Arabic without realizing they had abandoned English, and by extension, the rest of the family. When they realized they had switched languages on us, they would burst out laughing together. When they laughed, they looked like sisters. Their laughs were so similar, echoes of what I imagined their mother to have sounded like.

When we were little, Angelica and I wished we had a secret language like Mom and Aunt Arwa. We longed for access to a set of sounds that only the two of us could understand. We wanted to be able to have secret conversations at the kitchen table in front of everyone.

At one point we even made up a language. We

gave it a simple name: "J" language, J for Jax and Josh. We were the only two fluent J speakers on Earth. Our language used the sounds of English with a few deep-throated sounds we had heard when Mom spoke to Aunt Arwa in Arabic. The hard *kh* sound was our favorite, like trying to dislodge a stubborn kernel of popcorn from the deepest part of your throat. Josh and I started a notebook to record vocabulary. We used the English alphabet plus some made-up hieroglyphs, and we agreed to hide the notebook under my mattress, as if the words in our language were jewels to be guarded.

"I'm not interrogating," Aunt Arwa said. "Josh said we could talk about it. It's his choice, not yours."

"First of all, it's *her* choice," Mom said. "Second, she's not going to say no to you. She's too polite to tell you to back off. So I'm doing it for her."

"Really, Mom," Angelica attempted. "I love that you're ready to do battle for me—really—but I don't need protecting. I can speak for myself. Besides, it's only Aunt Arwa. She's family."

"Tell me this," Mom continued to her sister, ignoring Angelica's plea for a voice. "How long have *you* known?"

Aunt Arwa frowned.

"Known what?"

"That this is who you truly are."

"Oh, stop it, Rana. Don't be ridiculous."

"I'm only asking the same question you asked before."

"It's not the same," Arwa said. "I'm an adult.

Josh is a child—very mature for his—for *her* age, I'll grant you that, but a child nonetheless. Ultimately it's Josh's life and Josh's business, but as a member of this family, don't I have the right to share my thoughts? I want to understand this. I can't do that unless we talk about it."

Dad was staring at his plate when he spoke.

"Angelica," he said. Silence. The wall clock seemed to tick in slow motion. "She doesn't go by Josh anymore. She's asked to be called Angelica. We should respect that."

Aunt Arwa seemed frazzled.

"I'm sorry," she started, looking to Angelica for forgiveness. "I told myself on the plane not to use the name Josh—but it's not easy to snap your fingers and change something as ingrained as your nephew's—niece's—name. Names are a huge part of our identity."

"I agree," Angelica said. "But you changed yours when you got married, didn't you?"

"I suppose I did," Aunt Arwa said with a smile. "Fair point. I see your mother has imparted to you her skills for witty comebacks. And your father is absolutely right, by the way. I need to make a better effort to use your new name. If I call you Josh, correct me. I won't be embarrassed. I'm old but I can still change my ways with a little practice."

She put down her fork and laid a hand on Angelica's arm.

"Listen, honey. I love you. I just want what's best for you. Maybe I'm old-fashioned but I don't think boys should wear lipstick and dresses, that's all."

"I'm not a boy."

"Well—okay. But your grandma didn't even let *me* wear lipstick when I was your age."

"I guess my mom's cooler than yours was."

Angelica was right. Our mom was pretty cool, relatively speaking. She loved Angelica. That was clear. But love didn't mean Mom was okay with having a trans daughter. She had known for a whole year now, and on the surface, she seemed fine, especially in front of Aunt Arwa. But as progressive and with-the-times as Mom sold herself to be, Angelica's coming out had rattled her to the core. It was obvious because it had rattled me too. I saw it in her eyes and in the way she would sometimes look nostalgically at Angelica, as if something she had loved dearly was gone. Though I sometimes felt it too, Mom and I never spoke of it, both too proud and too ashamed to admit it.

Mom wished she could be as cool as Aunt Arwa thought she was. But here's what Aunt Arwa didn't know. A few days after Angelica came out to Mom in the red dress, I found Mom crying alone on the living room couch.

"I would have been fine if it had been anyone else's kid," she told me, makeup running. "I would have been perfectly fine."

That day, I sat on the couch next to Mom and cried with her, not knowing where the tears were coming from. We both loved Angelica. We both loved Josh. We were happy for them.

Through our tears, we both kept insisting everything was fine.

* * *

"You've got to love Aunt Arwa," I say, running my hand over Katu's arched spine. "She actually ended up making Angelica her prom dress—stitched it herself and mailed it to the house. Can you believe it?"

Dad chuckles.

"Boy can she and your mother argue."

By now Ms. Jakintsu has taken a good deal of black sand out of the container and sprinkled it across the table.

"What are you doing with that?"

"Is from my beach."

I try another question.

"What exactly is it that you do? For work, I mean."

Katu leaps from my lap onto the table and walks to Ms. Jakintsu.

"You went there once, to my beach, by accident," she says. "You remember black sand? Warm sun?"

She's prying into my head, unearthing a buried memory.

"You still have scar, yes? Hiding in your hair?"

"Okay. Honestly. How do you know all that?"

"You remember when you were falling?" she asks, her eyes glowing like a teacher leading a student to an epiphany. "Remember warm sun? Waves? My beach? You remember all these things?"

She takes my palm and puts some black sand inside. I haven't thought about the black sand in years—my refuge between fainting and waking.

"Your sister is lost," she tells me.

"No she isn't. We know where she is."

"I no mean her body, that is in hospital. I mean her piece of soul. This is lost, pushed outside."

"What does that mean?"

"Our soul can be beautiful garden, if we want it that way. For this, must to give water, sun, and pull weeds forever. Always work, never stop. With age we get more wisdom, more beautiful flowers, but we also get more hate, more prejudice, more weeds in our garden. Is very hard work to keep our garden nice, no time to be lazy."

Dad keeps quiet. Is he also thinking about the beach?

"So where is Angelica? Where is her piece of soul right now?"

Ms. Jakintsu looks down at the black sand.

"On my beach."

I wish Dad would chime in.

"She's in a coma," I remind them. "My sister is lying on a hospital bed. I saw her this morning in the ICU. I understand the psychological benefits of using metaphors at times like these—flowers, gardens, beaches and whatnot. Maybe that works for you, and that's fine. But I can't do that right now. It doesn't make me feel better to think about Angelica in the abstract."

"Tell us about my beach," Ms. Jakintsu says, dismissing my wish to speak concretely.

She and Dad lean forward and listen.

"When I was there—on the beach—it was after I'd fainted in the bathroom."

"So for you," the old woman says, "the beach was for waiting."

I try to stay grounded in whatever semblance of reality I have left.

"I see your point," I tell her. "You mean the beach is a place you can go to when you're unconscious? Like me when I'd fainted or now for Angelica in a coma?"

"Maybe, yes."

"A place between life and death?"

"No between. Outside."

I can't tell if she means anything by that or simply has a problem with prepositions.

"So Angelica's waiting there now? On the same beach where I was?"

"Her piece of soul is there. Her body is in hospital. They disconnect."

"Well how do you propose they reconnect?"

I wonder how long Ms. Jakintsu can keep pretending there are answers to every question. It's like talking to a religious zealot, an ardent atheist, or an astrophysicist.

"Angelica will stay there until the world will

change." The old woman pushes some sand across the table. "Our world no is safe for her. So she waiting on my beach until we change it."

Not the quick-fix answer I had hoped for.

"Excuse me, Ms. Jakintsu," Dad cuts in formally. "I know I usually don't pay for our meetings, but this one was unplanned."

His mention of money yanks me from my train of thought.

"Kyle, is no problem. I had already make tea before you come. This is most important appointment today. We talk about Angelica now."

"Yes, thank you, and I would like to pay you for it."

He takes out his wallet.

"No need! Stop this talk. Focus."

"I really must insist that you take some form of payment," Dad says.

His voice has moved from polite to pushy.

"Kyle, what is problem? This no like you. Speak your mind."

For once, I'm on Ms. Jakintsu's wavelength.

Dad looks nervous. He rubs his eyes hard and runs a hand through his black hair.

"I want to pay you because I need more than a consultation today. I'm not here to talk about theories or beaches. Jax is right. We need to focus on something concrete. We need you to intervene."

Katu's ears perk up. His glowing green eyes examine the old woman's reaction.

She stands up and shuffles over to her ceramic turkey figurine.

"No," she says with her back to us. "Too risky."

"I'm aware of the risks," Dad says. "That's why I'm offering payment. I'll be as generous as you want."

"I no like that magic, Kyle, is dangerous, money or no money."

I wipe my forehead realizing I am starting to sweat. Ms. Jakintsu comes back to the table and sits down. Dad leans toward her.

"Please," he says. "We don't have time for the world to change. I won't let your beach of black sand become my daughter's new home. I thank you for letting her take shelter there when she needs it most, but she can't stay. You told me once that the beach is a refuge, not a home. Angelica belongs with us, here in New Haven."

"I already tell you," Ms. Jakintsu laments. "Angelica is waiting for change. When Jax went to my beach, he stay short time. Physical pain will come and go. For Angelica, is different, so much more than pain in her body. The way people are thinking need to change, the world no is safe for people like her. Angelica has coma because of this world. Why should she come back to it?"

"Because she's my child and I love her," Dad pleads in a rare display of emotion. "I'll do anything, no matter the cost. *Anything.* Name your price. I don't care. Please. Just help us!"

Ms. Jakintsu takes a slow sip of tea, swallows,

and expels a long sigh, like Mom might do. She slides the black sand off the kitchen table into the container and seals the lid. Katu meows and walks coolly out of the kitchen, like he knows what's next.

"Come with me," the old woman says, standing once more from her creaky wooden chair. "We follow Katu into living room."

CHAPTER SEVEN

The living room is a world unto itself. Unlike the kitchen, this classical Victorian chamber offers no bright walls or hanging plates. Apart from the huge flat screen TV, the room is wildly formal and perfectly preserved, like a period room at a museum. Panels with twists of flowers and vines flourish in the woodwork. Candles stand tall in dusty corners with tears of cold wax hardened midway down their sides. A straw owl perches wide-eyed near a lamp. Overhead hangs a tarnished chandelier with golden strings of crystals dangling in dim light.

Katu curls up on the ottoman. Next to him is a marble fireplace, above which I am shocked to see a painting I know well.

"Manet's *Argenteuil*," I let slip aloud. "I can't believe it."

Ms. Jakintsu half smiles, just like the woman in the painting.

"Is very popular, Manet. Many people like. This one, very nice. I love expression for this woman. She have big secret in her heart, easy to see, hard to explain."

"It's Angelica's favorite painting," I tell her. "We have a smaller version at home."

"In your bathroom, yes," Ms. Jakintsu adds omnisciently. "Now sit, please. We talk business. I explain how can you help Angelica."

Dad and I sit side by side on the couch. Ms. Jakintsu nestles down near Katu on the ottoman. As I look around, the room's smaller details come into focus.

Hand-carved patterns in the hardwood seem to dance. The mantle is cluttered with candles and stones big and small. On the far end is a faded bronze goblet next to several remote controls.

Ms. Jakintsu pets her cat.

"I have many years, am very old, no energy like before. This can make dubious result."

Dubious. Two points for vocabulary!

"Tell me," Dad says. "Is time still equivalent? Is there a good trade balance right now?"

She sighs like she has understood the question and hates the answer.

"Like world economy, this have big change in recent years. I no can promise nothing for time trade. Markets are unstable these days. Time no is equal for trade anymore."

"So what is it?" Dad asks. "One day for two? One for four? What's the going rate? Give me a ballpark figure."

"Ballpark? What is mean ballpark?"

"Never mind. Just give me an estimate on the going time trade rate."

"This is depend on your energy and generosity of spirit," the old woman answers, her half smile fading. "Time exchange is maybe one day for two, maybe one day for three hundred. No can say."

Once again, I am an ignorant guest in their intricate world.

"What exactly are we talking about?"

"Going back to save Angelica," Dad hurries. "Pay attention."

"Going back where?"

"In time, Jax. Have you not been listening?"

Everything makes sense to him. I suppose it would. It's his reality.

"What did you mean about time being equivalent? And a trade balance?"

Katu hops off the ottoman, crosses the floor, and jumps into my lap, as if to calm me down.

"It's complicated," Dad starts, searching his brain. "I don't know—it's like—you remember when you were young and you would ask what I did at work? Every answer I gave led to another question. This is like that. Maybe Ms. Jakintsu can explain it better."

Doubtful, but she clears her throat to try.

"For this magic," she says, "essential things are heart and power. You have heart."

I assume she is not referring to Captain Planet.

"And power? What's that?"

"Power have two kind: inside and out. Inside power, this like all memories you collect to keep someone in your mind. Think like math: one plus one plus one make three. You add memories, you have more complete picture of someone. Before, when you tell me story of Thanksgiving and Aunt Arwa, this is one memory, one piece of your complete brain picture for Angelica."

Dad nods, adding: "Like beads on a necklace."

"Or," Ms. Jakintsu says, "like child playing with *canicas*. Kyle, how you say?"

"Marbles."

No hesitation.

"Imagine young child, she drop big bag of marbles and all marbles go to every place in this room," the old woman starts. "Some marbles go under couch, under chair, in fireplace. Maybe one marble escape into kitchen. These marbles are your memories of Angelica, and this house is your brain. Brain is messy—memories roll here and there, hard to find, moving around always."

"Actually," Dad says, "the brain is set up more like a series of pathways or roads than like marbles. When you look at how electrical signals fire—"

"Too much," Ms. Jakintsu interrupts. "We keep marbles to compare. Easy to understand. So like I say, you must to collect these Angelica marbles in your brain."

"All of them?" I ask. "That's crazy. I have so many memories of her."

"For this magic your father want—this risky magic—we need just some important marbles, no all. Then we go to next step."

If this is a dream, I can't pinpoint when I would have fallen asleep. The day has felt seamless ever since Mom told me to meet her at the hospital. Maybe I fell asleep at the teachers' room table and Mom's phone call was the start of the dream. And maybe I'm getting sick. I do feel a tickle in the back of my throat. Whenever I'm sick my dreams play out like sinuous anxiety-inducing adventures—like Dorothy's trip to Oz. Every step leads to another. Every open door leads to a more complicated room.

"You said there are two kinds of power," I remind our hostess. "Inside power is our memories. What's the other kind?"

"Outside power," she says, walking to the mantle and fetching the bronze goblet.

The cat looks intrigued.

"This power is belong no to you but to our world outside—wind, water, dark, light—this power is every force who can affect us from outside."

"You mean the elements?"

"No always physical force."

"So more like vibes?"

"What is *vibes*?"

"I mean like energy?"

"Is part of our soul, how to explain…"

Not the soul pie again.

"You're saying outside power is a life force?"

"Goodness, Jax. How you love to give name for things! Today we call it outside power, this name is enough. Too many names for same thing."

Something tells me if her grammar were perfect I would still be confused.

"So," I start, "in order to save Angelica, we

need to combine our collective memories of her with all the invisible forces of the universe? Sounds easy."

She smirks as her chestnut eyes widen.

"No need *all* forces of outside power—just one. One will come here to us."

"Which one?"

"No can say."

"How do we get it to come?"

"We build inside power. When you have high inside power, the outside power will intersect with you."

"And when that happens?"

"Then," Dad cuts in, "we can go back in time."

Back to square one. I am more confused than before. The couch feels light under my weight. Am I floating? I feel light-headed, thirsty. When I woke up this morning, this is not where I imagined the day would lead. But here I am. Angelica was attacked last night. She didn't expect that either. Now she waits in a coma of black sand. Plans change.

My phone says 12:31 p.m. No updates from Mom. Dad looks at me, impatient.

"Do you understand, Jax?"

"I'm still not sure what you meant about a time trade."

"For payment. We can't just go back in time without paying for it. That would be stealing. If we can conjure enough inner power for Angelica then one of the outside forces might intersect with us. When that happens, we'll be given a deal."

"What kind of deal?"

"Can't know until it happens. We'll have to buy our way back in time when the moment comes at whatever price we're offered. It's not our choice."

I don't like the sound of that.

"How do we pay?"

Dad sighs from exhaustion.

"Time, Jax. We pay with time."

"What?"

"If the outside force that chooses to intervene is generous then we may be able to buy—say—one day for the price of two, or one for three. That would be a great deal. But Ms. Jakintsu said the exchange rates are pretty lousy these days."

"Whose time is being used for payment?"

Dad and Ms. Jakintsu exchange a glance.

"Good question," Dad says. "Luckily Ms. Jakintsu is an experienced negotiator."

"What if we don't like the deal?"

"We can't back out once the intersection happens."

I'm starting to see why Dad offered so vehemently to pay Ms. Jakintsu. It's risky magic, for us and for her.

Katu rubs his soft head against my arm.

"No can predict," the old woman says, tracing a wrinkly fingertip along the surface of the bronze goblet in her lap.

"You'll do your best," Dad says to her. "And I accept full responsibility. Use only my time as payment.

The intersecting outside force can have as much of my time as it wants. Leave Jax out of it."

"No is easy like this, Kyle. Outside force no always listen to what you want. This is why we say *outside*. Half your life come from outside, no control. Some good, some bad. Just luck."

Katu cranes his neck to face his keeper.

"Is there any way to help our odds?" I ask, looking for loopholes in the magic. "Any way to ensure we get a good deal?"

Ms. Jakintsu looks at me and smiles.

"Heart."

"Excuse me?"

I can't tell if she was clearing her throat or speaking English. She turns to my father.

"I worry that power of your son is too small. This is dangerous. He maybe bring bad force to intersection."

What does she mean my power is *small?*

"Jax has to be involved," Dad insists. "We have different memories of Angelica. And you know I can't trust mine. Half the things I remember aren't real. Honestly, I should go get my wife at the hospital. She would maximize our inner power. Rana has the most memories of Angelica, starting with kicks in the womb."

"The two of us will be enough," I say quickly, unable to imagine Mom coming here.

"Your father is right," Ms. Jakintsu tells me. "Your mother can help, is necessary more inner power for good intersection. Too many missing marbles. Bring Rana here is more safe."

"My mother won't leave the hospital. The hospital is *her* reality. If we go there to get her, we won't be able to come back here. Trust me."

Through her half smile Ms. Jakintsu looks skeptical of me, like when we first met this morning.

"Tell me another story," the old woman says, glancing at a clock on the far wall. "We have time."

"What kind of story?"

"Like Thanksgiving story. You build inner power, collect marbles—important memories that reach from brain to heart."

I look to Dad, at a loss. Memories of Angelica? There are hundreds, thousands. The air is electric as my brain scrambles to summon one at random.

Angelica and I tried out a new Thai restaurant in New Haven last week. I close my eyes and reimagine the evening. The walls were bright green. I remember because my socks were also bright green and a student at school earlier that day had remarked upon my choice of color. Angelica ordered flat noodles with tofu. I forget what I ordered. Massaman curry? Pad Thai? Odd that I should remember her order but not mine. While we were eating, Angelica told me one of her colleagues had just gotten laid off.

That's not the kind of story Ms. Jakintsu is looking for. At least I don't think so.

I dig for older memories, ones Ms. Jakintsu might want to hear, but my mind is blank. Memories hide in corners, sealed in cracks and crevices. So many marbles, so little time.

My eyes look down to the wooden coffee table in front of me—a simple trigger.

Just like that, a lost marble is found.

* * *

I was visiting Angelica in her freshman year of college, meeting her new friends, sitting with them on the floor around a dorm room coffee table.

The lights were off and the music was on low.

"It's *inside*, you idiot."

Mei was educating us.

"But isn't the whole area just sort of generally called the vagina?" Eddy asked. "Is this really a stupid question?"

"There are no stupid questions," Mei said. "Only stupid people." She typed something into her laptop, her face lit up by the glowing computer screen. "The dictionary defines *vagina* as 'the moist canal in most female mammals, including humans, that extends from the cervix of the uterus to an external opening between the labia minora'. So that means it's *inside*, Eddy."

"And moist," he laughed.

Mei shuddered.

"Why does the word *moist* sound so weird? Or is that only me?"

Eddy grabbed Mei's laptop and began typing.

He cleared his throat and spoke like an announcer.

"The word *moist* comes from Middle English *moiste*, from Latin *mucidus*, and means 'moderately or slightly wet; damp; accompanied by or connected to liquid having high humidity—"

"That'll do," Mei said. There were chuckles, then a lull. Then Mei continued. "You guys want to hear something weird?"

"Always."

"I probably thought of this because you mentioned Latin. In social studies class my sophomore year we learned about Aurelia Cotta in a unit on the Roman Empire. Aurelia was Julius Caesar's mother. Anyway, I kind of had—fantasies about her."

"Like…sexual?"

"Yeah."

Angelica laughed. She was right next to Mei, very close.

"Was there a sexy painting of her in your textbook or something?" Angelica asked.

Mei blushed.

"No, but she was hot in my mind. We hooked up on her chariot more than once."

"Weird," Eddy agreed. "But hot. I wonder if Freud said anything about having anachronistic fantasies."

"Maybe I was breastfed too long."

"Or not long enough."

"Or while my mom was watching the History Channel."

"Couldn't you have just gotten off to the living like a normal person?" Eddy asked. "There are plenty of hot girls whose hearts are still beating, probably even some chariot drivers. Actually, that sounds like a fetish people would pay big money for. Especially if whips were involved."

"Not the point," said Mei. "I don't have a chariot fetish—at least I don't think so. Could be subconscious. But fantasies aren't about someone you think is hot. It's a scenario that plays out in your mind, exactly how you want it to—but you know it never will. It's something that can only take place in your head because reality won't allow it. That's what makes it fantasy. The best part is you get to keep it all to yourself."

"Unless you share it with your friends around a coffee table."

"That *used* to be a fantasy of mine," Mei told Eddy. "I've got new ones now, and those will remain unspoken, thank you very much."

"I, for one, had no problem fantasizing about the living," Eddy said. "Jennifer Lopez, Jennifer Aniston, Jennifer Connelly…a lot of Jennifers, actually."

A laugh and a lull. Then Eddy spoke again.

"What about you, Angelica?"

She jerked her head toward him.

"Me?"

"Were you into Romans too or were your tastes more modern?"

"My fantasies, you mean?"

"Unless it's too weird to talk about with your brother here."

Angelica looked at me. Eddy was right. It was a little weird.

"Jax doesn't care," she said.

Angelica pondered the question in the candlelit darkness.

"Catwoman," she said at last. "I was obsessed with Batman, had the comforter to prove it. Jax can attest."

I nodded.

"And there was also Buffy," Angelica said.

"The vampire slayer?"

"Who else? But with Buffy my fantasy wasn't so much sexual as envious. I wanted to *be* her. I mean— don't get me wrong—it was sexual too. And sometimes we were both vampires. Just the idea of going after someone's neck—never mind."

"That's twisted, and please don't stop," Mei told her with a wink.

Angelica laughed. She was laughing at herself in the same way Mom and Aunt Arwa laughed at themselves. Dad never laughed at himself. I don't think I did either.

"It's hard for girls to find heroes," Angelica said. She was scratching at her ruby-slipper fingernail polish. "Not just superheroes but regular people who are heroic. Buffy was that for me—at least for a little while. The show had high and low points. The whole

Angel obsession was a bit much. But good writing or bad, I always enjoyed her neck."

On the coffee table in front of us sat a hot glass pipe of smoked weed and a half-empty box of wine. I looked around at Angelica's new friends. These people were the first in her life who had befriended her as Angelica. They never stumbled over pronouns. As a subject, Angelica was *she*. As an object, she was *her*.

It was November, so these people had known Angelica for three months, a short enough time for friendship to still involve constant discovery but long enough to feel like you have known each other for years.

But they had never known Josh, my brother. There was no part of Angelica they had had to "come to terms with", no slow and hard-fought acceptance of truth, no perceived reversal of reality. Their friendship was organic and pure. They liked her and she liked them, simple as that.

"Why Buffy, do you think?" Eddy asked. "Other than the fact that she's hot."

I was glad to be listening. Her friends' questions, though uncomfortable for me, were shedding light on a side of Angelica I didn't know.

Angelica was looking off into the darkness when she answered Eddy.

"I'd sketch scenes of Buffy in the margins of my notebooks—not always from the show, just scenes I'd imagined. I was her, she was me. I had her boobs, she had my face. Sometimes we'd hook up, other times we'd hang out. There were no rules. I had no control over what we said or did. It was spontaneous. I'd be somewhere—usually in school. No one else would be around. Like, one minute the bell would ring, we'd get out of class, and when I got to my locker, no one would be there. Then Buffy would just show up and ask about my day. Sometimes we'd make out, sometimes not."

Angelica had a Buffy poster in our bedroom. Mom and Dad assumed it was a young boy's obsession with a sexy actress. Why wouldn't Josh want a half-naked picture of Sarah Michelle Gellar on his wall? Mom and Dad didn't seem to mind, and neither did I—the actress, or the show.

In *Buffy the Vampire Slayer*, Buffy moves to a small town with her mom to start a new life after messing things up at her old high school by burning down the gym to kill vampires. But as it turns out, her new town is even worse. It's built over a portal to Hell. Luckily, Buffy is not afraid to walk through dark alleys and kick the ass of anything that dare emerge from that portal. She's just a girl trying to survive, balancing schoolwork with her duty as the Chosen One to battle the forces of evil.

No wonder Angelica loved it.

"You're not alone," Mei told my sister after a sip of boxed wine. At this point Mei had scooted even closer to Angelica. "When I was in high school I had a few dreams I was Buffy. It was something about her power—but also that she was so weird and could own up to who she was, you know?"

Eddy laughed.

"That, and she was hot."

"Shut up."

"Seriously," Eddy went on, "why are so many main characters these secret freaks? They're all in the closet about something, living double lives: Buffy, Alex Mac, Doug Funny, Harry Potter—and the vampires from that new series—what's it called? You know, the one you see people reading around campus lately?"

"*Twilight*?"

"Yeah, that's it. The vampires are pretty self-loathing in that, aren't they? Don't the good ones feel ashamed of their need for blood and opt for animals over humans? When did vampires become morally conflicted?"

"I don't know about *Twilight*, but Harry Potter's different from the other characters you mentioned," Angelica cut in. "He's got problems and enemies for sure, but he's not an outcast. He's famous. People adore him. He's a legend. Doug Funny was only famous in his mind. He didn't have any superheroes to look up to, so he became his own. It's genius."

Mei lit up with a goofy smile.

"Oh my God I effing *love* Quailman. That would be an awesome Halloween costume!"

"But Angelica," Eddy said with a frown, "Harry's not in the wizarding world the first eleven years of his life. His aunt and uncle make him sleep under the stairs. It's only when Hagrid tells him he's a wizard that it all starts to click. He was feeling abnormal because he *was*."

"I guess," Angelica conceded. She sounded like Mom—hating to admit that anyone else could possibly be right. "Still, it's hard to feel bad for anyone who finds out they're a wizard. Talk about a convenient ticket out of a sucky reality."

"But he never truly gets out of his aunt and uncle's clutches," Eddy reminds us, assuming we all know the series as well as he does. "They're his legal guardians. He has to go back every summer. It's a perfect way of showing how children aren't free. Even wizard kids are powerless to the world of adults."

"I know, and that sucks, but his real parents left him a bunch of gold," Angelica shot back. "Hogwarts tuition? No problem! One minute he's poor and his life sucks and the next minute he's a rich wizard. Why does he have to complain so much? He's such a brat. I'm sorry, I just can't feel bad for him."

"Doesn't that make his character believable? There are tons of twisted-up kids. Many are bratty."

"I just think Harry Potter makes being abnormal sound fun, which is misleading."

"Maybe, but Harry definitely becomes a great character in book five, at least."

"Oh my God," Angelica said. "Book five Harry is the *worst*. He's like—hey guys, I'm just gonna go fight all the Death Eaters and rescue Sirius alone, see ya later! He puts everybody's life in danger. So arrogant. I wanted to reach into the book and slap him."

"Exactly!" Eddy said, lighting up. "By the end,

Harry finally sees he's flawed and can make stupid decisions, even as the famous Harry Potter. He has to find a way to balance being the Chosen One with being human."

"Like Buffy."

"Like Jesus."

Angelica smiled, looked down, and stared into the coffee table like it would give her something clever to say.

"I guess he never really stops being an outcast, as a human or a wizard. He never truly fits in."

"Harry Potter or Jesus?"

We muffled our drug-induced dormitory giggles. An R.A. could be on patrol.

"Main characters are made to be outcasts so people can identify with them," Mei announced like a sage, putting a hand on Angelica's thigh. "Even the most mainstream people can feel like outcasts. There's always pressure from society to be someone you're not. There's just more or less pressure depending on how close to the norm you are."

Eddy was watching her intently.

"Some fit in ninety percent and feel ten percent pressure," Mei went on. "Others fit in five percent and feel ninety-five percent pressure. It's a spectrum. No one fits in a hundred percent. You can only approach it."

I was trying not to hate her. Mei had given me no reason to. But I couldn't listen to her without being annoyed. She seemed self-important, like she always had answers, like there was no question too abstract or complicated to be answered immediately. It felt like the conversation was a lecture, like she was waiting for all of us, the students in her class, to voice our opinions so she could synthesize everyone's ideas.

"Wait a minute, Mei," said the other guy across the table whose name I had forgotten. He, like me, had kept quiet through his friends' bantering. "If you're saying it's a spectrum, and that no one fits in one hundred percent, then how do norms get started?"

He was blowing his own mind.

"Think about it," he went on, each word its own brilliant marijuana-powered light bulb. "Shouldn't there be someone who fits in perfectly with the norm? At least one person? Otherwise, where's it coming from? Who's it good for? It's like making all people wear shoes too big for everyone's feet."

Angelica opened her mouth to speak but Mei cut her off.

"I don't think the norm is what's actually normal," Mei said. "It's just an idealized vision of what—of how things should be, because they're not that way. But maybe they used to be. And could be again. A mix of nostalgia and hope, you know?"

Without having time to know whether that made sense, Eddy chimed in.

"It's like the way old people falsely remember the past when they tell you everything was better when they were young. Didn't they have polio and segregated schools and no internet? How could life have been better in their day than now?"

"I think they seek refuge in the good ol' days when they're angry with progress," Angelica said. "But as soon as young people complain, they get angry and remind us how much harder life used to be for them, how we don't appreciate our luxuries—which we don't, of course. But that's the point. You want progress to become normal-feeling at some point. Women couldn't vote a hundred years ago. But women today vote without batting an eyelash. We take it for granted, and I think it's *good* we feel that way. It means we've completely cemented a new norm into our psyche. That's the true goal of progress."

Eddy laughed.

"My grandpa goes back and forth hating on modernity and the way life used to be. He says the world's going to hell in a handbasket, but he also says when he was young he had to walk to school every day, five miles in the snow in ratty shoes, dirt poor and dead tired from backbreaking chores. Why did they have so many freaking chores back then? At what point did everyone stop living on farms?"

"Now the boomers dominate the electorate," Angelica said. "They collect Social Security and hate the Welfare State."

"We have such conflicting ideas about what's expected of us," Mei said vaguely. She was now rubbing the inner part of Angelica's thigh. "There's so much bull shit to sift through."

"Mixed metaphor," Angelica told Mei, giving

her a playful elbow in the ribs. "You can sift through grainy things—like flour and dirt—but if you're talking about bull shit you'd probably have to wade through it, not sift."

"Unless the bull shit was dry and crumbly."

"Touché."

"Oh, you two," Eddy said with a grin. He paused, then opened his mouth again. "What is reality anyway? We're half made of genes, half made of commercialism, inside and outside forces that combine to produce us—and we're slaves to both. I don't know. It just feels like there's a 'real me' somewhere behind all of society's onion layers. Like, where's the line between who I truly am and what culture has shaped me to be? It's confusing. Like vaginas."

"Eddy, you're the only one confused about that."

Mei and Angelica laughed.

It was easy to see how Angelica had become fast friends with these people. They were witty and open-minded. I couldn't keep up. I wasn't one to light candles, get high, and psychoanalyze myself and society, but I was happy to see that Angelica had met some decent—

"Jax? Hellooooo?"

What? What? They were all staring.

"Who, me?"

They laughed.

"Yeah, man. You've been pretty quiet over there. What do you think?"

It was Mei who was asking. The teacher had called on me. I had tried to remain the student hidden in plain sight. Now, a deer in the headlights, I wasn't sure how much of the conversation I had missed.

I only wanted to know if Mei was hooking up with my sister. Why was I so petty? Who cares? It was none of my business, and yet, if Angelica had fallen for someone, I wanted to know—though I was still deciding whether or not to hate Mei. But that didn't matter. I wanted to know that Angelica trusted me enough to tell me; that's all. Then again, maybe she *was* telling me. How much clearer could it be?

My mouth was dry as cotton. I sipped some wine. My lips parted to speak. Nothing came out. I scratched my head. When I tried again, a waterfall of words came gushing.

"I'm at like eighty-five percent—on the normal spectrum, I mean," I directed to Mei. I held eye contact, not remembering what her question had been. "There were times in high school I felt weird. Everyone does. But I was pretty much the norm. I've never felt pressure to be anyone but myself. I'm comfortable in these plain blue jeans." I could tell I was rambling. I felt like my dad, mucking up with wordiness an explanation of something crystal clear in my mind. "I don't mean I like the jeans because the material feels nice—which it does—I mean I feel good in them. Myself. Confident. That seems dumb. Why should clothes make us feel emotions? They're just protecting our bodies from the elements. Why give so much meaning to them?"

A vision of thirteen-year-old Josh wearing that red dress, the day Mom met Angelica.

"Maybe blame is a spectrum too," I went on. "The same as your norm spectrum. So I'm eighty-five percent to blame when I feel good and others don't. Because maybe my comfort is tied to their suffering? Or maybe it isn't and none of this is connected and we're all just our own islands floating through life, half made from genes and half from commercials."

The guy whose name I couldn't remember was gawking in my direction.

"Is it just me or is anyone else hungry? Where's the number to that Chinese place down the street?"

I sipped my wine. Angelica was now holding Mei's hand under the coffee table, their fingers interlocked. They were smiling. And then, just like that, so was I. My sister was happy, so I was happy. For the first time in my life, it felt clear to me that the fates of people were bound together. Smiles had the power to prompt smiles. Tears could prompt tears. What other forces were at work among us? We were not separate islands floating in a vast, uncaring ocean; we were beads on the same necklace.

Eddy was calling to order Chinese takeout.

"You know," Angelica said to me and only me. "I could really go for some of Mom's kosheri."

CHAPTER EIGHT

Dad looks out the window.

"What on Earth is that noise?" He rubs his temples with both hands, smoothing out the wrinkles in his mind. "Do you not hear that low rumbling sound? Like an engine. Did someone leave their car running?"

Ms. Jakintsu and I look down at Katu, who purrs like an idle motor. Dad's cheeks go red.

"Of course. Sorry." Dad looks at his shoes and clicks his heels together like Dorothy. "It's just that sometimes a noise like that for me can be distracting."

"No must to explain. We understand."

I change the subject, addressing Ms. Jakintsu.

"You know Angelica used to go by Josh."

The old woman blinks twice, waiting for more.

"Did you also know you're part of the reason she chose the name Angelica?"

For once, the old woman seems surprised.

"Your father never tell me this."

"Angelica said you gave Dad a root mix from your garden, from an angelica plant."

Her eyebrows crinkle.

"No, I no remember this."

"It was some kind of mixture you apparently said would protect her." Ms. Jakintsu's face is blank. "That doesn't ring a bell?"

"Bell?" the old woman asks in confusion.

"You don't remember that?" I rephrase. "The angelica root from your garden?"

"I never have angelica root in my garden. I know this plant, but I never have. Funny you say this because my mother, people in our town would call her Arantxa, short name. Long name Arantzazu. Spanish people in factory called her *An-hel-ica* because Arantzazu, this name too hard to say. So my mother was like Spanish Angelica."

I turn to Dad.

"Angelica said you brought the mixture home and sprinkled it around the house."

"Don't recall," he mutters, still staring at his shoes, clicking his heels.

"Really?" There's nothing lonelier than being the only one with a memory, the sole keeper of a marble. Is this the feeling of hallucination? "Well anyway, that's how Angelica picked her name. She said she felt like the name was hers, like when she took it, she could finally exist."

Ms. Jakintsu stands up from her spot on the ottoman.

"Is wonderful when something have name. *Izena duen guzia omen da.*"

I nod without understanding.

"Good," she announces with a burst of vigor. "Is enough heart from you, I can see. Inner power is high. Take one of your hair and put inside."

The old woman holds out the bronze goblet.

"Put inside here. Hurry!"

She reaches down to Katu, whose fur floats off his back. A piece of cat hair is added to the goblet.

"Why add his hair?" I ask. "Does Katu have memories of Angelica?"

"Hair of Katu no is for inner power. Katu just going with you, as guide."

"We'll need a guide?"

"Many years ago, one client, rich man from Greenwich, he ask me to do this kind of magic, pay me big money. I no want to do because his mind is weak and his heart is small. But was late November, I have heating bills. This is very old house, high ceiling, expensive in winter, so I help rich man for money. I explain him inner power, but his purpose was greedy, which made big problem. After intersection he lost ten years of life in time trade."

"Wherever we end up, Katu will be with us?"

Ms. Jakintsu raises her eyebrows.

"Katu know how to come back home from any place, any time. He help you as guide. But this cat no have inner power, just fat."

She peers into the goblet.

"Turn this way," she says. "We face toward east window. Kyle, you too."

Dad nods absently, still focused on his shoes.

"I say words to bring balance. We bring together moon—" Ms. Jakintsu traces a vertical line in the air with her right hand, "—and sun." She traces a horizontal line in the air with her left hand. "Intersection of moon and sun, we call it *dana*."

Dad looks distracted, doing silent battle with his mind. I speak for us both.

"Is there some kind of spell? Something to bring us this *dana*?"

"Long ago, Christian police came in my town hunting for Jews, Muslims, and witches," Ms. Jakintsu says. Dad nods like he has heard this story before. "They knock on your door, make arrest, give you time to confess, time to blame other person in town. One nervous girl blamed her sister, sister blamed her mother, mother blamed neighbor woman she hated for personal reason. They force women to keep blaming women. After one week, almost every woman in my town was suddenly criminal. Christian police burned six of them alive. Other families had to pay money to government or go to jail. Some families moved away forever. Four hundred years later, when my mother was young, Franco told Hitler to test his bombs in Guernica, thirty miles from my hometown. Picasso made famous painting of this day. In one moment, bombs burned over one thousand people alive. So you see, all people for all times need *dana*. Now, Angelica is waiting for *dana* in our time."

Katu is alert. I wish Dad would pay attention. Ms. Jakintsu holds the goblet in one hand and stretches her other hand into the air.

"Magic is outside power in our world," she says. "I will try to use it now."

She closes her eyes, and out of her mouth, slow and steady sounds come forth: *Bagahi laca bachahe, Lamac cahi achabahe, Karrrelyos, Lamac lamec bachalyos, Cabahagi sabalyos, Baryols, Lagozatha cabyolas, Sam ahac et famyolas, Harrahya—"*

She turns to Dad.

"Kyle, pay attention!"

His head snaps up from looking at his shoes.

"What? Yes, yes, *harrahya*. I'm listening."

Ms. Jakintsu dumps the hairs in the bronze goblet in the fireplace.

"This no working."

"Yes, we're ready," Dad fires back. "I was distracted. Say it again. Please."

"Kyle, maybe you still see Josh and Angelica like different people, one before, one after. But she is one person. You and Jax must to concentrate on this."

Dad jolts upright.

"Josh, Angelica. I only feel love!"

Ms. Jakintsu squints at him critically.

"I can't lose her," Dad continues. "It's not an option. Look. I sprung this on you today. If there's nothing you can do then Jax and I should leave. If we don't have hope in magic then we'll go back to the hospital and hope in medicine."

With his final words, a light flashes in the fireplace. Katu turns his head in surprise. There appears the spectral image of a vertical crescent moon, followed by the glow of a circular sun. The moon and sun overlap, different shades of bright light.

"Is—yes—this is sign of *dana!*" Ms. Jakintsu exclaims, surprised by her own magic.

Katu's wide green eyes reflect the glow in the fireplace.

"Do you know what it means?" I ask.

Before she can answer, a violent gust of wind rattles the house and something smashes in the kitchen. Katu scurries off in panic.

We follow a worried Ms. Jakintsu into the still-fragrant kitchen where we find one of her plates in pieces on the floor, ceramic shards scattered like memories in a brain.

"Here, I'll help you clean it up—"

"Touch nothing!" she yells standing rigid in the doorway, her chestnut eyes filled with dread. "This no is accident."

I inspect the room. Nothing seems to have changed besides the broken plate.

"Was it a special plate?"

"No was special before, but is special now. Someone is come here, to my house."

"What? Who?"

"Maybe I invite him by mistake. I tell you I no am strong enough to control this magic!"

"Who have you invited? Who's here?"

I look to my father.

"Ms. Jakintsu," he whispers. "Was there a cow painted on that plate?"

He points to the mess on the floor.

"Yes," she tells him. "There was cow. Tell me, Kyle. Those people, those men who attack Angelica, this was at night when they attack, no? Late night?"

Dad nods, examining the ceramic shrapnel.

"Then of course he will involve himself!" she shrieks. "Why I no think of this before? Is very clear why he come."

"Who?" I ask, frantic. "Who has come?"

She continues to stare at the shards of plate on the floor. Dad does the same.

"He no show himself because now still is daytime, he hide—maybe in basement."

I'm too impatient to wade through her cryptic descriptions and choppy grammar.

"Dad, what on Earth is she talking about?"

"Gaueko," he says. And before I can ask more: "A force of the night."

"A spirit?"

"I'm not sure what to call it exactly."

"Here?"

"Yes. Soon. Or maybe already. Not sure."

I whip my head in all directions looking for clues.

"It's an evil force?"

Dad and Ms. Jakintsu eye each other. Neither wants to answer.

"Wait," I tell them. "What about the thing that just happened in the fireplace, before the house shook and the plate fell? Isn't the *dana* thing good magic?"

"Yes, but *Gaua Gauekoarentzat, eguna egunezkoarentzat,*" mutters Ms. Jakintsu. "Is necessary now to also respect domain of Gaueko."

"But it's still daytime. You said Gaueko is a

force of the night. It's not his domain yet."

I'm not sure I make any sense.

"Jax may be right," Ms. Jakintsu says, rubbing her chin. "We have double outside force intersection, *dana* and Gaueko. I never see this before. Always one, never two. Very strange."

"So there's a choice!" I say.

The old woman looks down. Something gives her pause. Her eyebrows furrow in confusion. She approaches the scattered shards on the floor and mutters something in her native tongue, squinting at the scene before her like a fastidious Ms. Marple.

"Ms. Jakintsu, can I ask what you're—"

"*Shhh*," Dad cuts in. "Let her work."

She squats down and leans close, her nose inches from the detritus.

"Letters," she says at last, though still looking puzzled. "These are letters here on floor, written in broken plate pieces."

Dad and I circle round to see what she sees. From left to right the letters on the plate fragments spell out: *odolbainogehiagogorria*.

"Crazy sentence," she says.

"The letters mean something to you?"

"Yes, maybe. Something like—*more red than blood*. But no is clear to me."

The phrase strikes a nerve, a memory: the sight of my own blood, the feeling of bare skin on cold bathroom linoleum.

"What did you say it means?"

"More red than blood," the old woman says. "No is making sense. This magic is foreign to me. Maybe you were right, Kyle. Time for you to leave before we bring more bad thing into my house. Go to hospital, see your wife. We finish this."

Dad's eyes widen.

"We can't leave now," he says. "The hospital is hopeless. Our place is here, with you. At least here we have a chance!"

"Kyle, is clear that love from one father, no one can count how big this is. But Gaueko is come to my house. He hide in darkness for you to make deal with him. This spirit, he know what you want. He know you will give him anything to save Angelica. He like this. It make pleasure for him. But no good is coming to you or Angelica from deal with Gaueko."

"Back up," I say. "Before, when you were looking at the letters on the floor, why were you talking about blood?"

She turns her dark eyes back to the shards.

"Letters say: *more red than blood*, like message to us. But why?"

I stand up and leave the kitchen for the living room.

"Come look!" I call after them. "The light is still in the fireplace. Let's use it. Let's go back and save Angelica before the other spirit gets here. We don't need him. Forget the broken plate. How do we make the deal with *dana*? Can we buy our way back in time?"

Dad stands with one foot in the kitchen, one in

the living room, torn, as usual, between decisions and worlds.

"Jax, do you remember when you fell and hurt yourself in the bathroom?"

I nod.

"When I found you, I think I was asking—"

"A question," I finish, as if our brains were fused, the same marble seen from two perspectives. "The letters on the floor—I know. I thought of it too. But it's got to be a coincidence. Or some random manifestation of your mind in this world. Ms. Jakintsu is right. It doesn't make sense. Like a bizarre detail in a dream. It could mean nothing. Or worse, it's a trap."

"Or it's a message," Dad throws back, exactly as I feared he would.

"Not everything has to be symbolic, Dad. We've come this far. Don't you hear Ms. Jakintsu trying to warn us? We don't want anything to do with this Gaueko character. The letters on the floor are meaningless. We're trying to make sense out of nonsense."

"But what if it *is* a message?"

"From Gaueko?"

"From Angelica."

Is he trying to push me out of this world and into another, deeper, stranger one? Worlds within worlds? Is this how his mind works? One door closes and another springs open? I've spent all my energy trying to accept *this* reality, one in which a woman named Ms. Jakintsu actually exists. A third reality—one that even Ms. Jakintsu disavows—is beyond me.

"Dad. Please. I can't follow you any deeper down the rabbit hole."

"I'm not asking you to. We've already hit bottom. We're trying to climb out. And we have two ladders to choose from. So will you listen to what I have to say? This goes for you too, Ms. Jakintsu."

She looks at me and shrugs.

"Yes, Kyle. We listen."

"Let's say the letters on the floor are a message from Angelica—from the beach."

Ms. Jakintsu's eyes light up. If she can handle Dad's logic, I might be able to buy it. I can't believe I'm depending on her to make sense of my own father.

"Is possible, yes, but no likely," the old woman says. "How you know this message no is from Gaueko himself? A trap, like your son already say."

"We know what the message means," he tells her. "It's an old memory that Jax and I share from when he was a boy. And it's a memory of warm sun, from your beach, far from darkness, well beyond Gaueko's realm. The message on the floor is not from him. It can't be."

I take Dad by the shoulders.

"You have a memory of me on the beach of black sand?"

"Yes."

Our realities fuse.

"So it actually happened? I was there?"

"Of course it happened, Jax. I saw you in the

sand. I was calling to you."

"I can't believe this."

"Now Angelica is calling to us through the letters on the floor."

Ms. Jakintsu looks skeptical.

"Explain me your thinking, Kyle."

"Angelica wants us to work with Gaueko. She's speaking to us through his broken plate. We have two choices: *dana* and Gaueko. *Dana* is a process, not a moment. It's long, drawn out, enlightened, beautiful— but it's a long path. Gaueko is just one night, risky and short-term but instant results. Angelica is telling us she doesn't want to wait on that beach for the world to change. She wants to be here to help push the world forward—even if that means risking more blood."

Ms. Jakintsu shakes her head.

"No good, Kyle. Maybe true, but no good."

He turns his attention to me.

"Think about it, Jax. When you woke up on the bathroom floor all those years ago, you woke up to pain and blood. The beach is sunny and warm, but it's Hell. You can't move. You can't *be*. Angelica wants to come back. Ms. Jakintsu, I want to make a deal with Gaueko."

"You know how risky is this?"

"We could get Angelica back tonight!"

"At what cost?"

Dad shrugs.

"I'll take whatever deal Gaueko will give me."

"Is dangerous to trust darkness," the old

woman says. "Even if Gaueko can help Angelica, no will fix bigger problem in our world. We need *dana* to find harmony or real problem will never solve. People need safety when they walk in this world, day and night."

"We're not changing the world!" Dad hurls back. "You're always thinking so big, which is admirable. But today we have just one purpose: saving my daughter. In one reality Angelica's in a coma. In another she's stuck on your beach. I hate both. So will you help us?"

Ms. Jakintsu looks down at the broken plate.

"Yes," she sighs. "We do your way."

They pause, not knowing what to say now that they agree. Then Ms. Jakintsu continues.

"You can go back in time before Angelica was attacked, save her before this horrible thing can happen. But I no can guess what Gaueko will want for time trade, is maybe cost you very high: ten years, twenty years. Even your life."

"What father wouldn't give up his own life to save his daughter?" Dad asks. "I'm ready for anything. Just make the deal."

I rush to interject.

"Dad. Wait. I'm part of this too."

He puts a hand on my shoulder.

"I can't involve you, Jax. You're young. Your time is more precious than mine. There's more of it for Gaueko to take. Besides, I won't sacrifice one child to save another."

"I don't care," I say. "Angelica is my sister. I'm involved whether I like it or not."

Dad dismisses me.

"I'll accept whatever terms Gaueko sets," he tells Ms. Jakintsu. "A day, a decade, my life. Beggars can't be choosers. But tell him to leave Jax's time out of it or the deal is off."

With that, the door to the basement creaks open. Katu, fat and orange, reappears with wide-open emerald eyes. He has been listening.

Dad tiptoes through the bits of broken plate toward the open basement door.

"I'm guessing this is the way?"

He leans forward to size up the staircase descending into darkness. Crossing the threshold, he starts down.

"Stop!" Ms. Jakintsu shouts after him. "Kyle, they go with you."

"What? Who?"

"Katu and your son."

"Absolutely not. I already told you—"

"You listen now, Kyle," she says sternly. "Is my turn to speak. I know Gaueko. This spirit hate one thing most of all: people who feel brave in darkness, people who go alone. He punish them. No is good to be brave. Must to be...you know Spanish word *humilde*?"

He nods.

"You bring Jax and Katu, you have better chance for helping Angelica."

Dad exhales.

"Fine, but if it's a question of whose time will be used for payment, only mine is to be traded."

"Leave me this problem," the old woman says, letting a half smile return to her wrinkly face. "I negotiate time trade, this is my job. I am businesswoman. Let me work."

"Thank you, Ms. Jakintsu," Dad tells her. "I can't thank you enough for all you've done."

"No thank before we finish, is bad luck!" the old woman says. "Now go. Follow Katu. He is expert for my basement. Remember two things, both very important: First, time travel is one way. No coming back after you go. Second, if you get lost, Katu always know how to find me again."

CHAPTER NINE

Where we are headed is pitch black. According to Ms. Jakintsu, we can't turn on the light. Starting now, we have to work inside the darkness.

Katu starts first down the basement stairs. Dad grabs my hand and pulls me forward. With each descending stair the temperature drops by degrees.

We reach the basement floor after fifteen steps. My head is hot, my palms are drenched, my stomach is twisted like a pretzel.

I speak with a shaky voice into the darkness.

"Ms. Jakintsu sounded nervous about the time trade."

"Of course," Dad says. "No one wants to do business with a spirit like Gaueko."

He pulls me forward through the dank room.

"How bad is this Gaueko character?" I ask. "Is he unlucky or just plain evil? On a scale of black crow to Satan, what are we working with?"

"It's unwise to place him on a Western spectrum of superstition—or to mock him when we need his help."

"Sorry."

Dad guides me by the hand through the basement, as if I were a little boy. I hear Katu walking nearby on soft paws. We have so far managed to avoid running into anything. I would like to find a wall. The basement shouldn't be wider than the house.

Then again, this basement could be atypical. If today has shown me anything, it's that I don't know very much. I wouldn't be surprised to find a hole in the floor two steps ahead of us, a pit where you fall back in time twenty years and land on a beach of black sand.

A spider web presses into my face. Thin lines of silk stick to my lips and nose like cotton candy. I wipe my face and claw at my shoulder blades to squish the sensation of crawling.

We come to a cold concrete wall. I hear Dad run his hand alongside it. I follow suit, eyes still unadjusted.

"What are we supposed to be looking—"

"A door," Dad answers impatiently. "We're looking for a door."

Katu meows off to the right. Dad yanks me that way.

"Is this—yes!" he exclaims. "This is it! Okay. You ready?"

Ready for what I don't know, but I hear Dad grab hold of the doorknob.

"Damn."

"Locked?"

We listen to the slow and steady drip of water falling on a pipe somewhere in the room.

"Ms. Jakintsu must have a key," I say. "Let's go back upstairs."

"There's no going back, Jax. We've already entered his domain."

"Dad, we made the choice to come down here. We can always go back."

"We have to speak to him."

"What? But isn't that Ms. Jakintsu's job?"

Dad clears his throat, ignoring my suggestion that we return to the light.

"Gaueko, my daughter was attacked by people who don't fear the night. They used your darkness to prey on her. They took advantage of your realm. Help us restore your dignity by letting us confront them."

No answer but the drip drip drip of water on a pipe in the darkness.

"Ms. Jakintsu is upstairs, waiting for you," Dad goes on. "She's ready to make a deal. I'm prepared to be generous. Please let us work in your darkness."

With that, the door clicks. Dad jiggles the knob again.

"It's open!"

Then we hear a noise from behind—a bellowing animal cry, disconcerting enough to stop Dad from opening the unlocked door.

"Was that Katu?"

Across the room a soft white light has illuminated the wall. The rest of the room is still dark. The light on the wall is not projected from any point that I can see. The wall is simply lit without a visible source, revealing a door.

At the base of this new door sits plump and orange Katu. He lets out another deep meow—almost a growl, a deeper sound than any house cat should physically be able to emit.

I turn to face Dad but can't make him out. He and I remain enveloped in darkness, side by side. We observe Katu and the illuminated door. I can feel Dad's uncertainty.

Suddenly, in front of the door, the spectral image of a vertical crescent moon appears, followed by the glow of a sun. The moon and sun seem to float, each existing inside the other to form a single image.

I grab Dad's arm and pull him with me toward the light.

"Come on!"

He jerks his arm free.

"No, Jax. That's *dana*, like upstairs."

"Stop resisting, Dad. This is the second time it's been offered to us. What would Ms. Jakintsu say? Even Katu knows it's best."

"Of course it's *best*," Dad replies near my ear.

I can feel his impatient eyes boring into me.

"If it's best, then what's stopping us?"

"I see the door, Jax. And I want to walk through it. But that way is false. Superficial. *Dana* is a concept, not a place. There's no door that leads to harmony. It's a long path and a lot of hard work, like keeping a garden free of weeds. Right now we're just looking at a door with symbols floating in front of it. Moons and suns don't mean anything on their own. Symbols only work when people believe in them. In our world, not enough people believe to make them real. At least not yet."

He's right. Angelica isn't behind that door. Her piece of soul has been pushed outside.

"There can be no future with Angelica unless we change the past," Dad says. "We have to prevent the attack in the graveyard. That means we go through Gaueko's door. Do you understand?"

"Yes."

He pulls me back toward the other unlocked door, away from the light, away from the empty symbols—the dream of harmony. Katu runs toward us.

I hear Dad once again grab the knob and turn. The door opens and we walk blindly into the night.

* * *

New Haven is brighter than a basement.

"Are we—I mean—did it work?"

I turn left, then right, trying to get my bearings. I check to see if my feet and hands are still there, that nothing has been lost or turned backwards. My face feels normal.

Dad lets go of my sweaty hand. When I turn around, the door is gone. Ms. Jakintsu's house is nowhere to be seen. We are now outside, close to Yale, a few blocks from the New Haven Green.

"Are we on Grove Street?"

"I think so, Jax."

Tombstones stand around us like forgotten souvenirs in the glow of streetlight. A pale full moon hangs in the empty sky, displaying its ancient face, the crater-carved half smile as mysterious as Manet and Ms. Jakintsu.

"Have we gone back in time?"

Dad tears his attention from the moon to look at me.

"This must be last night."

"How do you know?"

"It has to be," he says. "Why else would he bring us to this spot?"

"I don't get it," I say. "We're *in* the graveyard."

"What's your point?"

"Angelica was attacked outside the graveyard. Are we sure it hasn't happened yet?"

"If Gaueko agreed to Ms. Jakintsu's terms like we planned, then yes. But you're right. It is strange that we'd be inside the graveyard already, unless…"

"What payment did he take?"

"What?"

"Gaueko. How much time did he take from you? And how can we ever know—and—wait a second. How could we even be talking about this if we've gone back to yesterday?"

Dad seems annoyed.

"Wouldn't that mean we were never at Ms. Jakintsu's house?" I go on. "But we both remember being there. The memory's not gone. And Katu's still with us."

"Thinking chronologically won't help when you're traveling in time," Dad says. "Don't worry about the payment. That's Ms. Jakintsu's job. I'll find out the terms of the deal sooner or later—hopefully later. Right now we need to find your sister."

Mom said Angelica was attacked near the cemetery we are now standing in. It happened on Angelica's way home from work.

"I'm still not sure *when* we are," I say. "How do we know it's the right night? And how do we know we're even in the past? Could we have gone into the future?"

"Now you're just being ridiculous. Check your phone. What's the date and time?"

I pull out my phone.

"Okay. So we're back to last night. But what are we supposed to do about her attackers? We're not the strongest people in the world."

"*Shhh.* Did you hear that?"

"I'm trying to make a point," I say in the tone Angelica and I use when it's clear Dad's not listening. "Seriously, Dad. How do you expect to fight them off?"

"*Shhh.*"

Then I hear it. Someone is yelling for help. Katu sprints toward the source of the desperation with Dad and I close behind. We zigzag through a cluster of headstones, hopping over flowerpots and miniature American flags as Katu leads us toward the ever-loudening screams.

We emerge on a dirt path between rows of tall graves to see three men standing over a body. Two men are kicking. The other holds something long in his hand—a baseball bat or a pipe.

"Police!" Dad yells without warning. "Put your hands in the air!"

The attackers dart like panicked deer into Gaueko's darkness.

"Wow," Dad says with surprise. "Good thing that worked."

We hurry toward Angelica, who lies on the ground curled up like a fetus. Blood is smeared on her shivering face, but not nearly as gruesome as my memory of her at the hospital. We must have arrived before the worst could happen. Gaueko met us in the middle.

Dad pulls out his phone and calls 9-1-1. Angelica looks up in dismay.

"Jax?" she gets out in a hoarse attempt at speech. "And—*Dad?* Is that you?"

He nods with his cellphone glued to his ear. She stands up and brushes herself off while Dad gives directions to an emergency responder.

"Those assholes," Angelica fumes with both hands clutching her sides.

Her hair and work uniform are caked with dirt and blood.

"It's just—the things they were saying—*damn* that hurts—I thought they were just robbing me at first—back on the street—but then one of them hit me over the head. I must have passed out. Next thing I know they're dragging me in here—"

"It's fine now," Dad says, finished with his call. "They're sending an ambulance."

He wipes away the blood on his daughter's face. As soon as it's gone, more emerges from a deep gash in her eyebrow. Katu purrs and circles at Angelica's feet.

"How bad is it?" she asks, tracing her cheekbone with her index finger. "I must look like Carrie after prom."

Dad smiles.

"The blood matches your fingernails."

Angelica fans out her polished nails.

"They're redder than blood," she says. "And would you look at that—not a single one broken. Go figure."

The whine of a distant siren eases my nerves.

Angelica puts one arm over each of our shoulders and we help her hobble toward the cemetery gate. We can't leave like we came in. No door leads back to Ms. Jakintsu's basement. No wormhole back to tomorrow. Some things just aren't possible in anyone's reality.

Katu meows from twenty or so feet down the fence. Just beyond the bars on the sidewalk is a wooden crate. Angelica recognizes it and shudders.

"That's how they got me in here," she says. "Looks like one of those Yale dining hall crates from across the street."

Dad and I hoist Angelica to the top of the pointy iron fence.

"You good?" I call out.

She plants one foot on each side of the thick iron bars. Then, with both legs over, she slides out of breath down the fence to the wooden crate, then steps onto the sidewalk.

"I'm fine, I'm fine," she hurries from beyond the bars. "Just get out of there!"

I help Dad up next, though he doesn't need much support. He slips a little and bangs his arm on something at the top. It would be safer for us to wait inside and have someone let us out through the main gate. But then we would have questions to answer, starting with how we got in here.

Dad slides down the other side of the fence onto the crate, then to the ground.

Now alone in the cemetery, I scramble to get over the fence with what little upper body strength I have. Luckily, adrenaline is on my side. I climb up and straddle the top, looking back toward the graves half expecting to see Angelica's attackers rushing back to finish the job. Fear quickens my pace. I tear the skin on my left hand on one of the pointed bars. It must have been labor-intensive for those guys to get Angelica in here. What kind of people go this far out of their way just to hurt a stranger?

I slide down to the sidewalk, panting.

Katu is last to escape but his exit, unlike mine, is done with Bolshoi grace. He moves down the wall a ways, where a grave pokes out of the grass. The fat feline gets a running start and uses the gravestone as a springboard to leap over the spiky fence.

We walk to the closest street corner. The sirens are loud now, only a couple blocks away.

We wait across from Yale's Woolsey concert hall, kitty corner to the well-lit façade of Silliman College, the undergraduate castle of stone. The intersection's traffic lights are red. Pedestrian walk signs are on. No one here but us. New Haven is asleep.

Angelica sits down, sucking up her pain.

"So—like—what the hell were you guys doing out here this time of night?"

I knew the question would come but still hadn't thought up an answer.

"How'd you even get in the graveyard?" she asks. "The main doors are chained shut. And where the hell did this cat come from?"

Katu purrs and pushes his orange head into her leg. I open my mouth to improvise a lie but Dad cuts me off with the truth.

"We were with Ms. Jakintsu," he says. "She wanted us to intersect with *dana* but we went with Gaueko instead. It was risky but that's the hand we were dealt. You can't choose the outside forces that intersect with you. You can only make the best of things as they happen. We're not sure what our deal with Gaueko will cost me in time. But the payment doesn't matter. It was well worth it. You're safe, at least for tonight."

Angelica gives him a familiar smile, a light and easy "that's-my-dad" smile, the smile that forms when listening to the details of a senseless hallucination.

I have given Dad the same smile a thousand times but never noticed until now just how condescending it looks. The worst part is I always thought I was being nice. But it's ugly when someone you love is smiling just to humor you.

For once, Dad's reality matches my own. I have glimpsed at his world. He took me to Ms. Jakintsu's house. We traveled back in time to save Angelica. I want desperately for Angelica to know the truth—or at least what Dad and I experienced, real or otherwise. But she will never believe me. She can't. She would call it hallucination. And maybe it was. Maybe I entered Dad's mind, peeked around, and now I'm back—a window into his world that opened only briefly and now is closed. Anything is possible.

The ambulance pulls up. Two paramedics get out. They seem relieved the situation is non-life-threatening and help Angelica onto a stretcher.

"I'll be fine," she moans. "Jax, why don't you walk Dad home, it's only a few blocks. Then come find me at the hospital. Dad, I'll have Jax call you from the hospital. Just—when I call, make sure you tell Mom I'm alright. No need to send her into panic mode."

Angelica will expect the "real" story at the hospital. I will have to be creative.

Dad looks at his feet and clicks his heels, already somewhere else.

CHAPTER TEN

Unlit houses line our path. Katu crosses the street and heads toward our neighborhood. Dad and I follow, neither of us talkative.

My car is at home, in the driveway, not parked on Ms. Jakintsu's street where we left it. We have really gone back in time, which I suppose means we never went to Ms. Jakintsu's house at all. Or at least we will never need to go. Yet the old woman's cat remains. A glitch in the magic? A token to prove we weren't dreaming?

This is why Dad said to avoid thinking chronologically. It complicates things. All I know is many things have happened over what has felt like a very long day. The exact sequence of the happenings is not so important—just that they all happened. This must be how Dad feels every day of his life.

Katu struts into our kitchen as Dad opens the door. I head upstairs to check on Mom, who is sound asleep. She won't get a call from the hospital tonight telling her that her daughter is in critical condition—though that *did* also happen, maybe. But it happened in another world that is not connected to Mom's memory, only to mine and Dad's. Mom also won't have to call me to say that Angelica is in a coma. That will be a bad memory for me to tuck away, a marble to roll into a corner, collect dust, and hopefully never resurface.

Most importantly, Angelica got to leave the black sand. She swapped the beach for a few broken ribs, some cuts and bruises, and a hearty dose of humiliation. Not bad knowing what could have been.

Dad goes into the bathroom to brush his teeth. I walk in, stand behind him, and talk to his reflection in the medicine cabinet mirror.

"I'm sorry I doubted you." I wait for him to respond, but he keeps brushing. "I'm still kind of in shock about everything."

He swishes and spits out a mouthful of toothpaste.

"How did you say Angelica chose her name?" he asks, off topic. "Something about a mix of roots?"

"From Ms. Jakintsu's garden."

"Funny. I really don't remember. Are you sure Angelica didn't make that up?"

Dad brushes past me and walks down the hall to the bedroom he shares with Mom.

"Jax," he says before walking in. "I'll be waiting for a call from the hospital. Your mom and I will see you there in a bit."

He enters his bedroom and closes the door.

Something soft rubs up against my feet, giving me a jump. Katu, ogling me with those bewitching emeralds, meows once, then heads downstairs. I follow him to the door.

"Ready to leave?"

He meows again. I let him out. He walks to the car at the base of the driveway, then sits, turns to me, and meows once more. He wants a ride home.

It's last night. Technically Ms. Jakintsu hasn't met me yet. But that's absurd. She can't *not* know me while I still have her cat. Anyway, Ms. Jakintsu deserves to know that everything worked out with Angelica. And we need to know the deal she brokered with Gaueko. There's time for a quick stop before I meet Angelica at the hospital.

I occupy the driver's seat. Katu jumps into my lap, purring. I drive down our street, take a left, and head past the closed markets toward the woods. Leaf-blown roads lie paved and vacant. I recall the moonlit faces of Angelica's attackers in the cemetery. They are still out there, free. They could be anyone.

Katu curls up in my lap as I turn onto a street full of potholes and Victorians. I stop in front of the big yellow house sitting up on the grassy incline behind the hedge. Everything is like it was this morning: faded paint chipping and curling, mossy shingles sinking into the old roof, shutters blocking the tall windows.

But one thing has changed. Near the sidewalk in front of the hedge in plain sight is a sign: *FOR SALE.* No realtor, no phone number.

I pull up to the curb. When I open the door to get out, Katu springs from my lap and takes off in a sprint down the dark street, away from Ms. Jakintsu's house.

"Wait!" I call out in a strained half yell, conscious of the wee hour.

I run after him, stopping when the bulky ball of

orange fur disappears into the darkness.

I look back upon the big yellow house where Dad and I will never need to spend the day recalling memories of Angelica and plotting her rescue. My eyes will never see that bright ceramic turkey. My mouth will never taste those mussels. The container of black sand will never be opened. Ms. Jakintsu isn't waiting in a wood-paneled living room complete with chandelier, fireplace, and a print of Angelica's favorite painting.

None of it will happen. It doesn't need to. Because it already did.

EPILOGUE

How could this be—that I, alone, am left with the memory?

A month has passed, another moon. I have tried discussing it with Dad three times. On each occasion, his face went blank. He simply has no recollection of our trip to Ms. Jakintsu's.

For a whole week afterward, I couldn't believe that he couldn't remember. It felt impossible. That he could forget such a thing felt unfair, cosmically unjust, though I don't believe in cosmic justice. I know his brain is simply wired to forget. That's just Dad. It's who he is.

When I told him we had traveled through time to save Angelica, he laughed and said, "Watch out, Jax. You're talking like me!"

Still, somewhere deep in the caverns of Dad's disorganized brain is the memory of our trip into Gaueko's darkness. Perhaps the memory sits alongside the forgotten mixture of angelica root from Ms. Jakintsu's garden. Dad might remember it all again someday if exposed to the right stimuli, like he remembered calling out to me on the beach. All it takes is the right trigger, and someone else who believes you.

But some things get buried forever, perhaps for good reason. The brain keeps some roads open while others are shut down, too risky for travel.

Angelica remembers our coming to her rescue in the cemetery. That, she will never forget. What she doesn't know—and could never understand—is how we got there.

The night Katu ran away from me, Ms. Jakintsu's house was vacant. I haven't mustered the courage to return. I accept that I will never know the deal she made with Gaueko in the time trade. How many years of Dad's life were taken so that we could save Angelica? Two years? Twenty? As Dad said that night, he will find out sooner or later—hopefully later.

Part of me can't help but wonder if Ms. Jakintsu gave up her own time so Dad could keep his.

One thing, at least, is not in question. An assault by three men in a local cemetery left my sister bruised and broken. There is nothing ambiguous about hatred and blood. Cuts and scars are not cultural. Wounds are not figments of any imagination. Even now, Angelica's side still aches as her broken ribs mend. Her face is still sore from being punched and kicked.

But Angelica is here. She has a name. She exists.

* * *

It's Friday. That means garlic and tomatoes, lentils and rice. Kosheri night.

Our family has decided to make Friday night dinners a regular event. It was Angelica who suggested it. We are all busy with jobs but life is short—too short. So make time to eat with those you love.

After eating, I excuse myself and go to my old bedroom. I lie on my childhood bed, stomach sated and warm, and stare up at the rickety ceiling fan. I don't turn it on for fear of disturbing the layer of dust living atop the blades.

Suddenly, a word springs to mind: *khillup*. It's the word for *fan* in "J" language, the secret code that Angelica and I crafted while huddling together on the floor of this room. How that marble rolled to the front of my consciousness I have no idea. I haven't thought about J language in years. *Khillup* is the only word I can recall now. But we had a whole notebook…under the mattress!

With childish excitement, I leap off the bed and flip up the mattress—only to find nothing. I expected as much. Objects, like memories, don't always stay where you put them.

I lie back down and take in the room. The bedroom walls are still light blue. The soccer ball wallpaper curls at some edges but seems determined to stick forever, unwilling to warp with time. Angelica's Batman comforter is tucked neatly into her old bed, and a frayed poster of Buffy the Vampire Slayer is thumbtacked to the wall near the window. Buffy remains our guardian, watching over us, doing battle with the forces of evil while we sleep soundly at night.

No matter how old we get, this will always be our room, the sanctuary for all the store-bought props that kept us company through childhood—whispers of who we were, and who we are.

With my head sunk deep into the bed pillow, my body and mind are at ease. As I drift off—not fully awake or asleep—I feel my mouth forming the hint of a smile, not coy like the Mona Lisa's, but knowing, in control, like I've got something up my sleeve and everyone's about to find out what it is.

THE AUTHOR

Danny Stone grew up in Malone, New York. His other books are *Then Comes the Harvest* (2014) and *For the Love of Mary Brennan* (2012). Stone has two short stories published in *Queen City Flash* (2013). He lives with his husband in New Haven, Connecticut, where he teaches English to newly resettled refugees.